GALACTIC
WAR

RANDELL K. WHALEY

Black Rose Writing

www.blackrosewriting.com

The final approval for this literary material is granted by the author.

First printing

All characters appearing in this work are fictitious. Any resemblance to real persons, living or dead, is purely coincidental.

ISBN: 978-1-61296-175-0

PUBLISHED BY BLACK ROSE WRITING

www.blackrosewriting.com

Printed in the United States of America

Galactic War is printed in Times New Roman

INTRODUCTION

This story is pure fiction. There is nothing in it that is based on fact as earthlings would observe. If it appears to be similar to anything or any of the characters are similar to anyone the reader has known, it is purely accidental. It is about people on planets in another galaxy light years away from planet earth. The time era could be either millions of years ago or millions of years into the future, take your choice.

It is about what people can be expected to be like anywhere, but not necessarily how the reader might expect them to be like. While it would be classified as science fiction, it is intended to be and is different from any science fiction work this author has ever read.

Enjoy.

GALACTIC

WAR

CHAPTER 1
ESCAPE

He maneuvered his fighter spacecraft up alongside the wreckage that was floating in space. He used his retro rockets to pull to a stop. Then he got into his pressure suit and fastened on his umbilical line. He opened the inner airlock hatch, climbed through, fastened the other end of his umbilical line to the fitting outside of the inner hatch, and tightened it down again. He decompressed the airlock to save air and then he opened the outer airlock hatch and floated out into space toward the wreckage. He held onto his umbilical line and let the distance from his spacecraft increase gradually. There were bits of debris drifting in space that was spread out over a wide area. It was what was left of an enemy fighter spacecraft. It had taken a direct hit from a laser cannon during the recent space battle with the Rebel forces.

There was something specific he was looking for in the wreckage, a certain black box. Then he saw it. He played the umbilical line out some more so he could reach it. He wasn't able to grasp it because of the bulky fit of the gloves of his pressure suit but he managed to get hold of it by wrapping his arm around it. Then he tugged very lightly on his umbilical line and headed back toward his space craft.

Once back inside the ship with both airlock doors secured he removed the pressure suit and looked at his prize. It was the identification equipment for what had been a Rebel fighter craft. He wanted the code for entering the gravitational field for the headquarters planet for the Rebel Forces and the equipment for generating and sending that code. He also needed the coordinates to the Rebel headquarters planet. And here it was, in this little black box.

Ensign Vic Maloney was a fighter pilot for the Empire. And it was a very depressing existence. He felt like he was treated as little more than a slave. But his biggest problem was that he didn't like fighting for what he didn't believe in. It wasn't that he had any back off on fighting. It was just that he wanted to fight *for* what he believed in instead of *against* it. So he located his tools and installed the equipment in the cockpit of his own spacecraft. The black box included a small computer and he knew that that was where he'd find the coordinates of the planet he was seeking. That was the information he needed since the location of the Rebel headquarters planet, in itself, was a carefully guarded secret. No one in the Empire knew where the Rebel headquarters planet was located. They just knew that it existed.

When he reached the patrol boundary for the Rebel headquarters planet, he would be intercepted and shot down by anti-spacecraft missiles unless he could identify himself as a friendly spacecraft. And the electronic identification equipment would accomplish that. With it installed on his spacecraft, turned on and transmitting the right code he'd be mistaken for a Rebel fighter craft returning from a mission.

He got ready to enter the coordinates of the planet in his navigational computer but found the new black box wanted a password! He hadn't thought of that! All his hopes deflated immediately. And he really had thought that he had an answer to his problems. It still wasn't too late to resume his patrol and return to base. He just needed to wait until his relief arrived. But he was falling into a deep depression. He really had his hopes up and now they were crushed.

And what would he do with the black box? He didn't want to jettison it. It was just a lucky coincidence that it came into his possession to begin with. But he couldn't return to base with it in his possession, either! It would be found by the maintenance personnel if he left it in the space craft and found on his person if he tried to smuggle it out.

He turned back to resume the path of his patrol. He'd have to figure out what to do with the black box.

And then another thought hit him! He could take the computer completely down and start it up again and it would require a set up from scratch. Then it would prompt him for a new password and he could enter it. He tried it and it worked.

So he found the right screen and found the coordinates of the Rebel headquarters planet. Thankfully the auxiliary memory device on the computer wasn't affected by having to start it up again. He entered them in his navigational computer and changed course. Once he was out of his assigned patrol quadrant, he'd be a deserter and would be court martialed and shot if caught. So that would be the point of no return. There'd be no turning back. You know what? he thought. I'd rather *be* dead than go back. If he was going to die, it would be while fighting for something he believed in or, at least, while striving to get into position *to* do so.

His navigational computer indicated that it would take 5 hours to reach his destination. And that was only if he jumped off to warp speed. He could do that. His little fighter craft was not designed to maintain superlight speeds for long intervals of time. In this spacecraft, warp speed was used only to travel to a patrol area or to withdraw to return to base. Warp speed was useless during a space battle. You couldn't maneuver while at warp speed. The stress would tear the spacecraft apart if you tried to.

He made some fine tune corrections in his course before he went through his checklist for jumping off to warp speed. Then he opened the throttle to full speed and pulled her up to full sub-light speed. He placed his head back against his head rest, his arms on his arm rests, then pushed the little round button near his left hand. It was like getting blown out of a cannon. He re-tuned his view screen to make sure he had a good view of anything that might be in his path. He could make small corrections in his course while at warp speed but they had to be small changes and he had to start them soon enough. A collision with an asteroid would be fatal, of course.

His warp drive control stick was on the right arm rest, down near his hand. The sub-light control stick was between his legs. It was the most convenient place for a control stick in the erratic maneuvering needed in a dog fight. But the warp drive control stick was smaller and did not have the amount of travel to it as the sub-light control stick.

So he settled down to a boring 5 hour flight. 5 hours and 36 minutes to be exact. But while it was a boring flight it would be tedious because he'd have to monitor his view screen and make sure there were no obstacles in his path. He had already been on station for about 10 hours or so. So this would make it a 16 hour flight. He was accustomed to flying 12 hours each flight so an extra 4 or 5 hours shouldn't be so bad.

However, after about 4 hours of flying at warp speed, he started feeling a little weary. And that wasn't good. He needed to be especially alert for what was to come. He moved his arms and rolled his head around on his neck to keep awake. It was a process he had to repeat often but he managed to stay awake.

After 5 hours and 25 minutes it was time to go through his checklist to come back down to sub-light speed. Having something to do did tend to help wake him up. He knew he'd need some maneuvering time and he'd need to call in a preliminary report to the Rebel base while approaching it. Otherwise they'd determine he was an enemy and take defensive action. He had to appear to be in a damaged Rebel spacecraft which would explain why he was this late returning to base after the space battle that had taken place the day before. And he also needed to make it appear he was wounded.

After he managed to reduce his craft down to sub-light speed and saw the planet on his view screen he monitored his distance continuously. He was wide awake, now, and that was good at least. He'd need to give them a radio report and it would have to be given in Ultarian. That was no problem, since he spoke fluent Ultarian. Then he'd have to determine the exact distance so he could report his position and he'd have to somehow disguise his voice to be convincing. Then his stolen identification transponder would be transmitting and they'd pick up that. He should be able to get past planetary defenses okay. At least with luck, he should.

When he was nearing the orbiting altitude from the planet he fired his retro rockets to get his ship down to orbit speed. He smoothly maneuvered into orbit and then selected the frequency that the black box computer gave him. Now that he was busy he was all right. He made his report in a weak voice with a groan every word or two. So it should appear that he was badly wounded. He didn't want them to recognize that it was a strange voice talking to them and he knew that he'd probably speak in an accent they'd recognize as strange. He received an answer, asking him his state. He grumbled back that he wanted to make an emergency landing. The voice came back on the radio telling him to stand by for identification. His identification transponder should still be transmitting. He certainly hoped it was.

After forever, the voice finally came back and told him he was cleared for an emergency let down and landing. He noted the coordinates the voice came from. He'd need that to find the location of the base once he was inside the planet's atmosphere. So he set the coordinates in his navigational computer and fired his retro-rockets to get below orbiting speed and started his letdown. It was night time on this part of the planet and he knew that would help. They wouldn't recognize his craft as being one of "The Empire" nearly as soon this way.

Then he sighted the Rebel base and the landing pads. The landing pads were lit up. He had been cleared for landing on pad number 32. And he didn't know which landing pad that was. Oh, well, if he just landed on one of them he'd get her on the ground. They still thought he was flying a damaged spacecraft and that he was wounded.

So he pulled into a hover, about 1000 feet from the surface, reversed his direction, adjusted his view screen for the rear view so he could see the landing pad as he approached and took her on down to a smooth landing.

After he touched down, he went through his secure checklist and shut down all his drives. Then he unstrapped, got out of his seat and headed for the entrance hatch. They should have a ladder attached by now. He climbed out, went down the ladder to see four Rebel guards with blast rifles aimed right at him. Flood lights lit up the landing pad. He finished descending the ladder and immediately raised his hands and placed them on the top of his head. They indicated that he march in a certain direction. After they were clear of the landing pad there were street lights to give them adequate light. It appeared that they didn't speak Armenian. That was fine. He did speak Ultarian but no need to tell them that, at least not yet.

Vic was medium height and medium build except he had broad shoulders. He had dark brown hair and blue eyes. He was 22 years old but looked like he was in his late twenties.

CHAPTER 2
THE NEW EMPIRE

They directed him into a stone structure with a double gate. They ordered him to halt. They had to wait until someone opened the gate. Then they marched him inside and into the building. Then he found himself walking down a long passageway with steel bars on both sides. About halfway down the passageway, there was a soldier waiting just on the other side of an open cell door. Vic walked calmly into the cell and they locked it behind him.

So, he had made it this far. And that was good. If they had recognized him flying an Imperial spacecraft when he first approached the planet they would have sent interceptors out to shoot him down. And if they had recognized him for what he was when he was approaching the landing pad, they would have shot him down with anti-spacecraft fire. The fact that he had survived this long meant that he had a chance.

He had been at space for about 20 hours. He had spent about an hour going to his patrol station. And he had been on patrol for 10 hours or so. But with the extra time he had spent salvaging the recognition equipment he needed, the flight to the Rebel headquarters planet, then orbiting and landing took another 8 hours in all. And it normally took about 3 hours or so from the time he got up until he could actually get spaceborne what with briefing, preflight checks, etc. So he had been up for over 20 hours.

There was a bunk in his cell and he pounced on it. It had a soft mattress. And there was a pole with hooks on it that looked like it served as a clothes hanger. There was a dim light in the cell block. As soon as the guards left he removed his clothes and turned in. The bunk had clean sheets, a blanket and what felt like a feather pillow. So when he laid down and got settled he was out like a light. He slept soundly for 12 hours.

When he woke his throat was parched with thirst. He saw what looked like a water jug just inside the cell door. So he got up, put on his clothes and then went over to investigate. He pulled off the cap, tilted it up and tasted it. Yep, it was water.

He must have drunk half a gallon of water before he finally succeeded in quenching his thirst. Not all at once. He drank a few swallows then waited a few seconds. His stomach started cramping. When the cramp dissipated, he took another slug. But after a few minutes the jug was half empty.

There was actually a chair in the room in addition to the bunk. So he made up his bunk and had it looking neat, just like he had to do in his quarters back at the Imperial Fleet base. He tried to arrange his flight suit as neatly as he could. Might as well try to make a good impression, he thought.

So he sat down in the chair and tried to relax. He checked his watch to find out it was about 9 PM. No one had come to wake him. Then he thought about how his watch had been set for Armenian time. So he actually had no idea what time it was. Well, he'd find that out soon enough, he guessed.

After he had rested up and then quenched his thirst he started feeling hungry. He hadn't even thought about hunger till now. Of course after he landed last night he had been so keyed up, wondering if he was going to be allowed to live, that he had forgotten all about being tired until he arrived at his cell.

"What are you in here for?" he heard a voice behind him.

He turned around to see a man in the adjoining cell. He was unshaven and his hair uncombed. Also his clothes were rather dirty and unkempt.

"Who wants to know?" was his answer.

"Call me Gus," was the answer.

"What are you in here for?" Vic asked.

"I was framed for burglary," Gus said.

"Regrettable," Vic said.

"Can you tell me what time it is?" Vic asked him.

"Well, yeah," Gus said, looking at his watch. "It's 5:43 PM, nearly time for dinner." So Vic set his watch. At least he had the correct time, now. Then he took a few moments to reprogram his watch to Ultarian time. Their time system was different than that on

Armenia but his watch was programmable.

Their conversation was interrupted by two guards that came by, one of them pushing a cart. It had a big pot of something and a stack of bowls and some cups. They stopped at each cell that had occupants, and one guard ladled out something into a bowl and then took a kettle and poured something into the cup while the other guard held a blast rifle at the ready. Then the guard opened each cell door, placed the bowl and cup inside on the cell floor while the other guard kept the prisoner covered, then closed and locked the door again.

When they reached Vic's cell, he just remained in the chair and didn't make a move until they opened his cell door, placed his dinner inside, then relocked it. He walked on over and picked up the bowl and cup and walked back to his chair. He looked in the bowl. It appeared to be some kind of stew and a spoon had been placed inside it. There was also a cup of hot herbal tea. Hot herbal tea was the standard drink for both the Empire and the Rebel forces. It was probably mediocre stew but it tasted delicious to him. He cleaned up the stew and drank the hot drink and would have been willing to have seconds if they'd been available. But he least he'd had a meal. He was grateful for that.

These were actually pretty decent accommodations for a prison. And that meant that they hadn't passed judgment on him yet, which was a good sign. He knew that the Rebel fleet would accept defectors from the Empire if they were convinced that they were bonafide. He knew there'd be a careful screening to make sure that he wasn't a plant. But he knew they were recruiting from other planets for their fleet. He had heard that from a black market trader he encountered on the street one time.

The next day he woke up and was brought a breakfast of corn mush and hot tea. He kept a comb in his pocket so he combed his hair and tried to smooth out his flight suit. Then after about an hour two guards came for him. It was about 9 o'clock. He was marched down the hall to the entrance of the prison building and back out the gate with the double doors. They then turned to the right down a concrete road. The guards walked one on either side of him and kept their blast rifles at the ready, but they didn't tell him to raise his hands.

There were buildings on both sides of the road. The road was made of what looked like asphalt and the buildings were just plain structures, like what you'd expect on a military base. The architecture was a little different than on Armenia. But they looked like what office buildings or barracks would look like.

The street was for the most part deserted. But then it would be if everyone was already at work. They marched him down the end of the road to a building that looked like it could be a headquarters building. The front of it was a veranda with two columns at the front and steps leading up to it on each end. They marched him up the steps and he saw a beautiful woman at the other end of the veranda watching him as he arrived at the top of the steps. She was wearing a long dress that went down to her ankles and had red hair. The dress was of a fine fabric and her hair was done up on the top of her head. She was a looker.

The guards ignored her and marched him to the center of the veranda where they had him turn left and enter the building. He pushed open the door and walked in. The guards followed. He found himself in a hallway. The guards motioned him to go through the first door to the left.

CHAPTER 3
THE ADMIRAL

When he marched inside he saw an admiral sitting behind his desk. He had on a khaki uniform with short sleeves and no tie. Above the left pocket were 6 rows of ribbons and a set of space wings above them. He had red hair, too. In fact, he saw a faint resemblance in the nose and eyes to the girl he'd just seen outside. So they must be of the same race, he thought. Vic simply stood at attention and said nothing. He decided that this was a time to do just nothing and speak only if spoken to. He had the feeling the Admiral was looking right through him.

The Admiral waited a full minute before he said anything. His two guards remained silent and seemed to be as much in awe of the Admiral's presence as himself.

Finally he spoke, "Lose your way home?"

"No sir," was all he said.

"It seems you deserted your own fleet." It was a simple statement.

"Yes sir," was all he said.

"You had to have had a reason," the Admiral prompted him.

"I'd rather serve *for* the Rebel Fleet than *against it*, sir. I want to fight *for* what I believe in." Then he was silent again, staring straight ahead.

"Are you applying for admission into the Rebel fleet?" the Admiral queried.

"Yes sir," was all he said.

"Why should I grant your request?" the Admiral asked.

"I'm a good fighter pilot, sir. If you need more fighter pilots."

"We always need more fighter pilots." the admiral stated simply.

Then he turned to an officer on Vic's left that he had been totally unaware of until now. "Major, swear him into the Fleet with the same rank he now has and get uniforms issued to him. Cut him a set of

16

orders to transition fighter training." Then he turned his attention back to the papers on his desk. The matter was closed.

The officer stood up and dismissed the guards. He escorted Vic out into the hall. He introduced himself as Major Gillette. Vic saw he had on a Fleet Marine uniform. He took him across the hall to his own office. He had him raise his right hand and repeat the oath of allegiance to the "New Empire". Then he had him sign his commission as an Ensign in the Fleet of "The New Empire." Then he told him his orders would be ready the following morning. He turned his head and told a non-rated man nearby to show him to his quarters.

He learned that the non-rated spacer's name was Sol and he took him down the steps and headed down the street, the same street in which the prison was located. If you could call it a prison. From the outside it looked like any ordinary barracks. But they went on past that building and two buildings down. They came to another building that looked like a barracks, too. They went inside. There was a duty officer at a desk just inside the front door and a lounge area with chairs and sofas and such. The duty officer also had on a khaki uniform with short sleeves and no tie. Sol introduced him to the duty officer as a new officer that had been assigned to space flight training. The duty officer assigned him a state room. Sol showed him to his room. He asked him if he had any luggage. He told him no.

Sol told him he would need to check out uniforms and gave him directions on where to go. Then he told him to report to the admiral's office at 10:00 AM the following morning to get his orders. Other than that he had the rest of the day off. Vic asked Sol where the mess hall was and he told him. Sol left him then to go back to the administration office. So Vic went to the supply building and got measured for his uniforms. After finding a working khaki uniform that fit, he asked the storekeeper if there was a place where he could buy a razor and toothbrush. He went to the base exchange and bought a razor, toothbrush and all the things he needed to make a shaving kit. When he started to pay for it, he found he had nothing but Armenian money. The storekeeper said he could sign a voucher to have it subtracted from his first paycheck. With that problem solved, he went back to his quarters. He'd pick up the rest of his uniforms later on in the week. He got a shower, shaved, brushed his teeth and changed to his khaki uniform. Then he went out to find the mess hall.

So, he was now an officer in the Rebel Fleet! Except he had noticed that they didn't call themselves the Rebel Fleet. They called themselves the "New Empire." And they didn't call the Empire the Empire. They called it the "Old Empire." They didn't consider themselves to be rebels. They were a separate confederation of planets with their own government and their own separate identity.

And all of this was very interesting to young Ensign Victor Mabry, of the Fleet of the New Empire.

CHAPTER 4
RED HEADED ANGEL

On the following morning, Vic reported back to the headquarters building to pick up his orders as scheduled. The red headed girl was standing just outside the door again. This time she was wearing a red miniskirt. It matched her red hair. She also had on red high heel shoes. They matched her hair, too. As he walked by he said, "Hello".

She smiled back with the most a beautiful smile he had ever seen and said, "How are you?" He felt like he was floating in the clouds just from looking at her.

He said, "I am fine," and went on inside. He picked up his orders and the other paper work that he would need to turn in at the flight school office. He also got a voucher signed to get an advance in pay. Then he walked back out. The red headed girl was still standing there. She looked so beautiful. He was awestruck again, but this time when he approached he said, "My name is Vic."

She said, "They call me Red."

He said, "I'd call you beautiful." She blushed, and then smiled again. It made him feel dizzy when she smiled.

"How would you like to go to lunch at about noon or so?" he asked.

"I'd love to!" she exclaimed, almost too quickly. It was his turn to blush now.

"I'm not familiar with the base," he said. "Do you know of a good place?"

"There's a snack bar right across from the class room building where you'll start ground school," she said.

"Okay, I'll meet you there at about noon," he replied and then he left.

He reported to the building where the ground school classes were to be held and completed his check in procedure. He found out that his first class would start at 1:00 PM. It was already about 11:30 AM or so. There was a clock in the hall. He checked it to make sure it was the same as his watch. He decided he'd go outside and see if he could find the snack bar that Red had told him about. He found it and found her waiting outside. She was early, too.

"I expected they'd let you go early," she told him. "So I came on over."

They went on inside and ordered lunch. So it was like as if he had died and gone to heaven and was now getting acquainted with an angel for the first time. He didn't know it was possible to feel this good. And she had a glow on her face that he didn't understand. It made her look stunningly beautiful. She just kept her eyes on his. Just stared at him completely unabashed. He stared back. She had beautiful green eyes. When the waiter brought his food he didn't even notice.

Then she spoke, "You'd better eat, Vic. It's going to be a long time before dinner." Then he noticed the sandwich in his plate for the first time. He picked it up and took a bite out of it. She did the same with her sandwich.

He asked her if she lived on the base. She said she lived just off the base. She explained that she was the admiral's daughter and that's why she went over to the headquarters building as often as she did. His jaw almost dropped perceptively when she told him that. So that's why her facial features were similar to the Admiral's! She smiled and said, "Don't worry. He wants me to lead a life of my own. But I like to drop by and see my father when I know he has a chance to talk to me. I never get to see him otherwise. I bring him hot tea sometimes. And I sometimes get to have lunch with him."

Then he remarked about how it seemed the Admiral just looked straight through him during his interview.

"Daddy has the 'power,'" she explained. "He can tell if someone is telling him the truth just by looking at them. He could tell you were being truthful and that's why he accepted you into the New Empire."

Then he said, "I've heard them use the term 'New Empire.' The Old Empire just calls us Rebels."

"Yes, that's true. But there's a reason we call it the New Empire. We don't consider ourselves to be rebels. We have a government of our own and a civilization of our own. And the term "empire" is actually a misnomer. We don't have an emperor like the Old Empire has. Our government is run by our Parliament. At least they are the ones that make all the laws and regulations. The one person that really runs both our government and the fleet is Daddy. He meets with the Parliament occasionally and they always accept his advice. He's never wrong and they know it."

Vic continued to just be amazed at everything he was hearing. They finished their lunch. Then he remembered he had no knowledge of how to get in touch with her. He asked her how he could call her. She gave him the code for her home message system. He memorized it. He explained he didn't know what time he'd get off work that night. If it wasn't too late, he'd call her that night.

She explained that it would be late. That he'd have classes all day and then simulator training that evening. It seemed like she knew more about his training schedule than he did. So he just asked her if he'd have his Saturday nights off while in training. She told him yes. Then he asked her if she'd like to go to dinner with him Saturday night. She told him yes to that question, too.

CHAPTER 5
LIFE IN ARMENIA

Vic's life hadn't been very happy up until now. He had graduated from the Imperial Academy only about a year previously. He had graduated from Imperial space flight training only two months ago. He had received his appointment to the Academy because his father was a loyal space fighter pilot in the Imperial Fleet. He never really knew his father. He was killed in action when Vic was 3 years old. And he almost never saw him even when was alive because he was always gone. His poor lonely mother did the best she could. But she died of a broken heart when he was 4. So he was raised in a orphan's home. Discipline was strict. If they so much as questioned anything they were told to do they were struck with a cane. They had bruises on their little bodies almost all the time. And as he grew older his resentment only increased. Loyalty to the Empire was all that counted. They wanted to conquer the entire galaxy. And they were told the entire galaxy had been conquered. But they were still at war. Why would they still be at war if the galaxy had already been conquered?

In his teens he continued his schooling. He was especially good at his engineering studies. He learned to keep his thoughts to himself. There were boys only at his school. It wasn't until in his late teens at the Imperial Academy that he even saw a girl. They would hold a formal military ball occasionally and they learned to dance. But at the dances the boys showed up for the dance in their full dress uniforms. Then the girls would march in. Each wore a mask over their eyes. They wore short shorts and each one had a nice hairdo and they wore dancing shoes. They'd pair off and dance. After the dance the girls would form a line and march out again. They never got a chance to get acquainted with them.

He was very reserved with his fellows. You never knew who you could trust. A sure way to promotion in the Imperial Fleet was to betray a trust with a friend. So he didn't try to cultivate friendships. There were times when he wondered why he was living.

His training was thorough. His mastered his studies in engineering. He was good at mathematics and science. And he also learned martial arts. He became proficient in all the personal weapons including blast rifles and pistols, light sabers and electric knives. But he also became very proficient in empty hand combat.

After he graduated from the Royal Academy he started space flight training. He learned quickly and was assigned to fighter craft. He was assigned a sector to patrol about two hours distance from the home planet of Armenia. They did spot Rebel forces on two occasions and attacked them. He wasn't proficient enough yet to score a kill. He just barely managed to avoid getting shot down himself. But after the first battle there were at least 6 pilots reported missing. And then he heard nothing more about it. No effort was made to look for them.

He put two and two together and figured out how his father had probably died. They didn't bother with search and rescue missions in most cases. They had the capability and would sometimes rescue downed pilots (it took too long to train them) but they didn't give it priority. So his father might have survived if they had bothered with searching for survivors. He had learned that the planet his father had crashed on had breathable air so he might have been alive when he landed.

He continued to fly patrol missions with his fighter craft. His job was mainly to report the presence of any enemy activity. The armament of his fighter craft was mainly for self defense. And he wondered why they bothered to provide them with armament since the lives of their forces seemed so unimportant.

It was after he had been involved in the second space battle that it occurred to him that there was a means of escape. When a space craft was destroyed in space the wreckage just floated there forever. He knew about the electronic identification equipment he used on his own space fighter craft. He figured out that the Rebel space craft probably had something similar. He had excelled in his electronic engineering courses in his studies. So while on a patrol mission by himself he had noticed the wreckage of the Rebel fighter craft and approached it and located the identification device. His plan had worked.

If he was ever captured he'd be executed by the Old Empire as a traitor and deserter he knew. But his real name hadn't been placed in the rosters of the New Empire. Sure he gave them his real name and it was recorded but he'd been commissioned under a different name than the one he had served under in the Old Empire. His name under the Old Empire was Victor Maloney. His commission in the New Empire was under the name of Victor Mabry. But his finger prints would identify him as Ensign Victor Maloney in the Old Empire.

So his new life now was like moving straight from hell to heaven. He certainly wasn't complaining.

CHAPTER 6
SMUGGLERS

The mountains of Armenia were protected by nature. It was not that Imperial troops couldn't be trained to be mountain soldiers. It was just that men that had lived all their lives or most of their lives in the mountains could easily evade trained mountain troops. They had hiding places where they'd never be seen. And they were good at hiding tactics which caused them to avoid being seen by anyone they didn't want to see them.

Smuggling was a booming business on Armenia and the guerilla troops provided them with a safe base of operations.

It began with the mountain men. They would trap animals and accumulate furs. And they would kill game for meat. They could live on meat alone for months on end, or years on end for that matter. But they didn't prefer a meat only diet. They liked the root vegetables they could trade for and the seed vegetables. And they all liked hot herbal tea. These were luxuries not to be had in the mountains without trading for them.

It was not practical to trade furs to the people in the villages and towns. Furs were illegal in the Old Empire. They would compete with the artificial furs and hides produced by the factories in the cities and towns that paid their taxes to the Imperial Government. Of course, they weren't going to sell their furs for the same price as the artificially made products. Also anyone who dealt in genuine furs were known to be members of or at least allied with the enemies of the Empire.

But the smugglers would buy all the furs and hides that the mountain men would sell them and take them to another planet somewhere and find a market for them. And they would pay them in any kind of currency they wanted, or gold or silver for that matter. So the mountain men would sell their furs and hides to the smugglers and use the money to buy produce from the villagers and farmers. They ate well.

Many of the mountain men were also guerilla troops, some of them only part time. But they were all friendly with the smugglers.

Another business the smugglers were engaged in was smuggling live bodies out of the Empire. Anyone who wanted to defect to the New Empire could do so if they went to the mountains and made their wishes known and came up with the required price. Of course, the guerilla leaders were alert to the possibility of spies and plants and were very reserved toward any potential defectors until they could do the necessary background checking on them to make sure they were bonafide. And the people wanting to escape from Armenia had to come up with their transportation fee. They'd have to come up with at least a thousand credits to pay for their passage.

Once their passage was paid for they were notified of a time and place to go to in the mountains. It would be a place in the foothills that they could find on their own without a guide. Then they would wait there for days. If Imperial soldiers were discovered nearby they might wait for weeks. But finally, after the guerilla officers decided they were safe a mountain man would be sent to guide them to their rendezvous. Or mountain woman as the case may be. They had mountain women, too. They dressed in animal skins and wore hats made of animal skin similar to the mountain men. In their shapeless garments you wouldn't know they were women just to look at them. But you could tell they were women when you saw them walking, of course. Women walk differently than men.

Once the defectors were determined to be genuine the guide would rendezvous them with the smugglers, at which point they paid their money and then were moved aboard the smuggling ship. Then they normally went to the planet Starkling first. That was the planet that had the facilities to sort through them and decide where to use them in the New Empire. Some of them would be permitted to join one of the armed services of the New Empire. But some of them, if they had a skill, would be assimilated into an industrial group as civilians.

It was a highly organized recruitment organization.

CHAPTER 7
GUERILLA OPERATIONS ON ARMENIA

Jules Stepps loved the mountains. He roamed the mountains alone many times. He made camp and slept wherever night fall found him. He loved the tall pine trees and the cold clear water of the mountain streams. He would either kill small game or fish in the mountain streams for his food. Sure, he accumulated furs during the winter just like any mountain man and would trade them for money to buy what he needed from the black market traders.

But he also would team up with other mountain men to strike at the Empire. The mountain men normally did not take the time for sabotage. To deal out death and destruction was not their way. But to find a means of permitting people to escape from the suppressive life that no one wanted hurt the Empire more than anything else they could do anyway. Aiding and abetting defectors was the main thrust of the guerilla movement in the mountains. Mainly to help political prisoners escape.

Jules was slight of build though he was medium height. He had a beard that was probably about an inch long and you could tell he didn't get regular haircuts but he kept his hair clipped so it didn't touch his collar. He usually just took a pair of scissors and clipped it himself. Long hair could snag on brush and bits of tree limbs. If you were standing close enough to him you might notice a little smell coming from his buckskin clothing but he did get himself a bath in one of the cold, icy streams every few days.

Colonel Aspen had been assigned the task of mopping up the guerilla forces in the mountains. He had been given a regiment of troops that had been trained in mountain operations. So it became necessary for the guerillas to fight in a more conventional fashion.

For now, Jules was assuaging his hunger with a breakfast of fish. The fish you could catch in a mountain stream were small. He'd usually catch at least three or four of them just for one meal.

He had roasted the fish over a small campfire. He scaled them with his hunting knife, gutted them, and then thrust a sharp stick through each fish from its mouth one at a time, then just held it over the fire until it was done enough to eat. Then holding the stick up to his mouth he just nibbled the fish off the stick. He did that with each of the three fish he had caught that morning. He'd have to spit out bones occasionally but that was no problem

The night before he had looked ahead to the morning and had fashioned a fish trap and put it in the creek, fastening it to both banks of the creek with two pieces of rawhide thong, each tied to a tree. He had built two cones of twigs, one smaller than the other. He placed the smaller one inside the larger one and put it in the stream. The inside cone had a hole in the tip so that when a fish went through it would swim into the outer cone and would be caught there. When Jules awoke at the first light of dawn, he built his fire and checked his fish trap to find his breakfast ready to be cleaned and cooked.

He had camped in a protected place where his fire could not be seen for more than 30 feet in any direction. There were spreading limbs above from the trees to disburse the smoke so it couldn't be seen. But a mountain man would know he was there. You can smell a campfire for maybe a quarter of a mile if there is any breeze. But the Imperial troops probably wouldn't smell his fire because of their own camp fire. After he finished his breakfast he climbed up to a mountain peak nearby to look around and see if anyone was in the area besides himself.

He saw a thin plume of smoke about a mile to the north and another about a half a mile or so to the east. That meant they weren't mountain men. You wouldn't be able to see the smoke this far if they were. He concluded that the one to the north was probably a refugee camp and the one to the east was very possibly Imperial mountain troops looking for the refugees.

He quickly broke camp, packed his supplies, shouldered his backpack and headed for the location to the north. He might as well warn them of the presence of the Imperial force.

He avoided trails but wound his way around fallen trees, rocks and underbrush. It took him about an hour to reach his destination due to the roundabout way he had to travel. When he arrived at the location where the refugees were camped, he halted on a ledge above them and studied them for several minutes before going down to approach their leader.

Jules moved quickly and lightly. He never got tired. He had lived in the mountains so many years that his body was so conditioned to moving in rough terrain that he was totally unaware of his body. He just focused his mind on the task at hand.

When the refugees saw him he seemed to appear magically in their midst. No one saw him approach. He walked up to the leader of the group and introduced himself as a member of the rebel force. The refugee leader introduced himself just as "Andre."

"There is an Imperial force camped nearby that will be looking for you," Jules explained.

"Do you know how many?" Andre asked.

"No, but you had better move out to avoid detection."

Andre turned and barked orders to several men who were apparently his lieutenants and they went amongst the men and women, urging them to pack their belongings and get ready to move out.

In fifteen minutes Jules was leading them up a steep mountain trail. After another few minutes Andre noticed that Jules was no longer among them. Then he appeared again at the head of the column of marchers and directed them down a new path as they mounted the summit of the mountain trail.

Nina was among the refugees and watched Jules as he led them up the steep mountain trail. She saw his quick, cat like movements. It appeared that it took no effort for him to walk up a steep mountain trail. And he looked so handsome in spite of his beard and animal skin clothing. He even had animal skin shoes and an animal skin hat, she noticed.

Nina was a beautiful young woman but it wasn't that apparent unless you looked close with the baggy clothing and the stocking cap she wore with her hair made up into a bun inside her cap. She had long dark brown hair and brown eyes.

At the end of the day, Jules had found them a place to camp that was well hidden and permitted them a small cooking fire.

"You should be safe here," Jules told Andre. "But it would still be wise to keep a lookout all night long to make sure no one can slip up on you."

"In which case, what would we do?" asked Andre.

Jules actually did not have an answer to that question since these were obviously people that had not been trained to fight. "Just avoid being caught by surprise." was the only answer he could think of.

Then Jules disappeared again. No one saw him again until morning. After they were up and ready to move out, he appeared and directed them down a trail.

Three days later Jules knew that he had led the group to a secure position at least 60 miles from the nearest Imperial force. He explained to Andre that they should now be safe if they remained in their present location until contacted by the guerilla soldiers or smugglers.

Then Jules left them and started toward the guerilla rendezvous point to advise someone of the new location of the refugees. He knew that no one would approach them until they had determined that there were no spies planted amongst them.

CHAPTER 8
GROUND SCHOOL

Vic reported back to the class room at 1:00 PM per his schedule, to class room 10A, to be specific. He found a seat. He had a jittery feeling in his belly. He figured it was just due to the new surroundings. He noticed the man sitting next to him. He had blonde hair and blue eyes and a twinkle to his eyes. Then the instructor walked in. He was wearing a khaki uniform and had the rank of an Officer Grade 3 on his collar. Someone called "Attention" as soon as he walked in.

"Take your seats," he told them. "My name is Lieutenant Ja Jahn." He then started his introductory lecture.

"The New Empire does not consider themselves Rebels," he explained. We are an independent confederation of planets that are self governed. We call ourselves the "New Empire" to distinguish it from the old, though we aren't really an empire in the true sense, since we have no emperor but are run by a Parliament, instead.

"Freedom for individuals and protection of the family are fundamental to the civilization we are building." This gave Vic a warm feeling because they were the two things that the Old Empire definitely lacked.

"The Old Empire continues to make war against us in an effort to win back the planets they have lost. The primary source of recruits for our cause are defectors from the Old Empire. And each defector has to have an interview with the Admiral. The admiral has a certain power that is very reliable. He can tell if someone is lying. So he can very consistently determine the reliability of each defector. If the Admiral determines someone is a plant, they are court-martialed as a spy, and if convicted, they are executed. If they are not convicted, we still can't let them go back where they came from because they could tell the intelligence forces of the Old Empire the location of the New Empire Headquarters which is a carefully guarded secret. It seldom happens, but if someone is tried and not convicted of espionage, they still aren't considered to be trustworthy enough for the fleet. So they are kept in a civilian capacity and they are watched carefully. If they turn out to actually be a spy, evidence will surface later and they can be dealt with accordingly."

Vic found it all very interesting and he was just glad all over again that he had succeeded in getting on board with the New Empire. And he noticed that as soon as the lecture started the jittery feeling in his belly went away.

At the end of the lecture, the instructor dismissed the class. Everyone came to attention in accordance with military protocol when he left the room. Then the instructor for the next lecture came in. His lecture was on the History of the New Empire. Vic learned that the New Empire got its start as a colony. The Old Empire had decided to colonize a planet that had a life support system but with natives that were very primitive. And the human population planet-wide was very low. So they built farms in the wilderness and built cities and factories. A space station was built for landing and or docking of cargo spacecraft and a flourishing trade was established. The rich soil produced good crops and the factories were manned by eager hard working people. Far away from the strict government of the Empire, they found they had a higher degree of personal freedom than they'd ever known before.

The agricultural and commercial enterprises on the planet Haven continued to flourish and prosper. The Empire levied taxes against everything they exported, of course. And everything imported, too, high taxes. The purpose of a colony was to provide profit for the Empire. That's how the Imperial government looked at things, at least.

Of course, smuggler ships found the planet and started buying their produce and taking them to sell on neutral planets and at a significantly higher profit for both sides than they could possibly get trading with The Empire. It wasn't long before the difference in the amount of cargo going to the Empire from Haven was detected. A force of Investigators was sent to the planet to find out why. They had with them a significant military force of combat ships, complete with a spacecraft carrier with fighter craft and strike spacecraft. No troops, yet.

The planetary governor, a gentleman by the name of Sir Rogineer Gallo, met with the Commander of the Imperial forces and explained he'd give them full cooperation in their investigation. Sir Gallo didn't want Haven to become an outlaw planet. He didn't want the strict suppressive environment that would result in military rule. He explained that the problem was the work of smugglers and he wanted to stop the practice of smuggling, too. And that he'd give them full cooperation in dealing with the problem.

The smugglers were promptly chased off by the strict patrolling of the space around the planet by the space fighters. They couldn't come in and land without being intercepted by Imperial fighter craft. They'd be escorted to the planet surface and forced to land and the crew placed under arrest and the ship confiscated. So the smuggling came to a screeching halt. But it was necessary to keep the military forces in control of the planet to prevent the smuggling from starting up again.

In the meanwhile, the personnel from the space ships of the Imperial Fleet would periodically come down to the planet surface for shore leave. And the Inspectors took up permanent residence at the various cities that had space ports with the necessary number of inspectors and police officers to make sure the smuggling didn't resume. It wasn't long before they found out they liked colonial life better than anything they'd ever known before in the Empire. When it came time to be rotated back to the home planet or to another theater of operations, they didn't want to leave.

Planetary defenses had been built to protect the planet from enemies of the Empire. Troops had been transported in to man these defenses. And these new troops invariably requested permanent assignment to their new duty stations. Haven was turning out to be a popular planet to live on.

The Emperor became aware of what was going on and saw the danger evolving. The Empire was at war with a confederation of planets and was limited to how many forces he could deploy to police existing colonies. But he saw the need to police them. So the Emperor issued an order for a major force to go and take control of the planet Haven and to investigate the "investigators."

All protective forces for the planet Haven were to be transferred to other areas in the galaxy and be replaced by the new forces. The existing forces refused to leave. A space battle resulted in which the existing forces defeated the Imperial forces and drove them away.

The planet Haven was declared a Rebel planet and more Imperial forces were sent against them only to find themselves in battle with Haven's defensive forces again. The war being waged to conquer new planets was starting to suffer due to the forces it took to squash the rebellion. So the Rebellion was allowed to gain a foot hold.

Three decades later, the Rebels had their own government and 10 planets had joined their cause. After another 10 years, 7 more colonial planets had done likewise. After another 35 years, the New Empire had a total of 137 planets. Since the government was a parliamentarian type of government instead of an empire, they decided they were no longer rebels, but had become a confederation of planets of their own right completely independent of their old masters. So the New Empire resulted. Vic was fascinated to learn all this. Very, very interesting.

The next lecture was an introduction to the spacecraft they would be flying. Vic noted a lot of differences between this spacecraft and the one he had been flying for the Old Empire. The size and maneuverability of it was about the same, but it was limited only to sub-light speed. It was intended only for planetary defense but it had the capability of operating from a spacecraft carrier. So it could be used while deployed to a remote location in the galaxy, if needed.

The remaining lectures that afternoon were about details pertaining to flying the spacecraft. Then at 6 PM they were dismissed for dinner with orders to report to the simulator training building at 7 PM. Dinner was at the chow hall and the food was better than Vic had been used to in the Old Empire. There was a kind of meat that he thought was delicious and two vegetables he didn't know the name of. But they tasted good. After dinner he followed the other cadets to the Simulator building.

When Vic climbed into the simulator and strapped into the seat he first noticed the similarities with the Imperial spacecraft he had been flying. The control stick was in the same place and so was the throttle. The switches for the protective screens were in the same place. No button for warp speed, of course. When the instructor turned the machine on and he started going through the flight procedures they'd learned in class, he noticed that the simulator was actually a better quality machine than the ones he had used in the Old Empire. They seemed to do a better job of simulating flight.

And Vic was starting to figure something out. Freedom for the individual was actually an environment that was more conducive to technological excellence. Everything he had experienced so far was a step up from what he was used to. People in the New Empire were obviously happier than anyone could ever hope to be in the Old Empire but they also were actually more highly disciplined and more productive as well. And he thought that was interesting.

At the completion of simulator training at 9:30 he returned to the barracks. He found himself following the cadets, though some were behind him also. There were about 30 or so cadets in his class. One of them looked over toward him and said, "What's your name?"

"Vic," he told him. Then he noticed he was the one sitting next to him during the lectures earlier in the day.

"I'm Dan Wilson. So you're from the Old Empire, huh?"

"Yes," was all Vic said.

"How different are these cans from the ones you've been flying?" he asked.

"Not too different. There are some differences," was Vic's reply.

So he had made his first friend. Dan was about the same height and weight as Vic. He had a square jaw and a big neck but had a pleasant manner.

"And where are you from? asked Vic.

"I'm from the planet, Solston. A lot of people from Solston join the New Empire. There are several other student pilots in this class that are from there."

They continued talking on their way to the barracks.

CHAPTER 9
RED

At the end of the week he start getting ready for his first date with Red. She had given him her address so when he changed to civilian clothes (which was permissible while off duty) he went out and hailed an air taxi. He told the driver the address. The air taxi let him off at her apartment. He went up to room 312, the room she had given him, and rang the door bell.

She opened the door and let him in. She was dressed in a deep blue mini skirt this time with blue high heels to match. And the mini skirt was really short. He was standing close enough to notice she wasn't wearing nylons. She had a beautiful complexion on her legs. She came up and gave him a hug. She had her hair down, just combed straight. It almost reached her waist.

"You really have beautiful hair," he remarked.

She blushed ever so slightly and said, "Men always like a woman to just wear her hair straight and plain."

"You are so right," he said.

They left her apartment and found another air taxi. They got in. He asked her to suggest someplace to go. He knew nothing about the area. She suggested the Ritz. So at the Ritz they had dinner: steak and a tuber vegetable that he found very tasty. And they also ordered some kind of drink. He just let her order and he ordered what she did. He wasn't familiar with anything on the menu. The drink apparently had alcohol in it because he felt a warmth in his stomach after taking several sips.

She wanted to know about him. He explained that his life in the Old Empire wasn't very happy. And that he'd rather talk about happy things. But she insisted that he should tell her something about himself so she could get to know him better. He then told her how his father was killed in a space battle when he was 3 and that his mother died of a broken heart when he was 4. She immediately started crying and then said, "Okay, I see what you mean. You decide what to talk about."

So he told her about his experience with class and simulator training and how refreshing it was to be treated like a human being. How great it felt just to be in such a pleasant environment. And that he was scheduled for his first training flight in a spacecraft on the following Monday morning. The bright look on his face while he described his experiences of the week brightened her up and she stopped crying.

After dinner she wanted to dance. So they got up and walked over to the dance floor. They danced until the place closed at 2 AM. Then they went out and found another air taxi. When he reached Red's apartment, he asked the air taxi to wait for him this time. He escorted her up to her room. He leaned down to give her a good night kiss at her door and then turned and walked down the hall.

When he got outside and climbed back in the air taxi he all of a sudden noticed that he had been in a daze all evening long. Just being in Red's company caused him to simply float in the clouds. And he now felt a sense of overwhelming loneliness.

He'd made a date with her for the following Saturday evening. He guessed he'd live until then.

CHAPTER 10
TRANSITION TRAINING

On Monday morning, Vic went to the locker room as soon as he arrived at the ground school building. He changed into his flight suit and went over to the spaceport where the trainer spacecraft were parked. There was a building beside the long line of parked spacecraft. He walked in and found the ready room. There was an orderly sitting at a desk just inside the door. He gave the orderly his name. The orderly introduced him to his instructor. A pilot named Lieutenant Davis. He was slender with gray hair. He looked to be in his forties. He was wearing a green flight suit the same color as Vic's. He started briefing him for his flight. He had an authoritative tone to his voice. He explained that they wouldn't leave the planet's atmosphere. They would just go joy riding. There was a space port away from the base about 10 miles or so where they could practice landings and take-offs. Just to familiarize him with the vehicle was the only purpose of this first flight.

They walked out and Vic started his preflight inspection. He walked around the outside of the spacecraft first and checked it over.

"What are you doing?" Lieutenant Davis asked him in an impatient voice.

"I'm making sure there aren't any defects in the hull." was Vic's answer.

"Now I don't want any lip!" was the lieutenant's reply. "Get up the ladder and into the cockpit."

Wow! thought Vic. What is with this guy? But he climbed up the ladder to the entrance hatch. The spacecraft was sitting on its tail, of course. Inside it had two seats side by side, but the seats were upright. They strapped in, with Vic in the left seat. Then Vic started the before start checklist. This included rotating the seat so they were lying back facing straight up, the direction in which they would take off. After starting the drives and completing the before take-off checklist,

Lieutenant Davis did the take off. Then when they were clear of the traffic in the vicinity of the spaceport he turned the controls over to Vic.

Vic noticed it did fly differently than the spacecraft he was accustomed to flying. It actually flew a little smoother. And it was more maneuverable, too. Mr. Davis directed him out to the practice landing port and Vic pointed the nose to the sky and eased her down to the launch pad very smoothly.

When they came to rest, Mr. Davis said, "You brought her down too fast! It's a wonder we didn't crash!" He had a harsh tone to his voice.

"Sorry, Sir," replied Vic. But he knew he didn't bring the ship down too fast. It touched the ground very smoothly.

Vic took off again to practice another landing.

"Keep your nose steady!" screamed the instructor.

Vic had the idea by now that there was no pleasing him. But he brought her down for another perfect landing. Mr. Davis couldn't think of anything to criticize him for that time. After about a half a dozen or so practice landings and practice take offs, they left and started cruising around the area. There was a range of mountains just to the east of the base. So Lieutenant Davis had Vic fly low over the mountains so he could get some practice compensating for up drafts and down drafts. It was also a beautiful view. And Vic found there was a huge lake on the other side of the mountain range. The name of the lake was "Big Lake," Mr. Davis told him. A very fitting name, Vic mused.

Vic noted that on the opposite side of mountains there was a town on the shore of the lake. It was a fishing village, Lieutenant Davis explained. Its name was Lakeside and its main industry was the fishing industry. Fishing boats came in off the lake and their crews would sell their catch to the fish processing plants along the shore. Then the fish were loaded into refrigerated gravity trucks and sent across the mountains to the fish markets and food stores in Oceanside. Mr. Davis' manner had calmed down somewhat since there wasn't anything especially to be critical of.

The presence of a market for fish also made Lakeside a favorite headquarters for the fishing boats themselves. Vic noted that there were piers and marinas all along the coast line to provide the needs of the fishing vessels.

They then flew back to the base and Vic brought her down and landed smoothly on the launch pad.

"A little better," the instructor remarked when Vic started his shutdown checklist. They walked into the ready room and Lieutenant Davis led Vic to a cubicle made for briefings and debriefings.

It was only a couple of flights before Lieutenant Davis decided that Vic was safe for solo. So he took a spacecraft out on his first solo flight. He just did the same things as before. He practiced landings and take offs at the practice space port and then cruised up over the mountains. Except this time he flew on over the mountain range and continued to fly out across the lake. It was a huge lake. It appeared to be hundreds of miles across and at least a hundred miles wide. He saw fishing vessels every so often as he flew across the lake. And he also noticed there was an occasional fishing village along each shore line, every fifteen or twenty miles or so. He noticed farms at the foot hills of the mountains on the lake side. They irrigated their crops from the mountain streams, his flight instructor had explained. And Vic learned that it was a fresh water lake.

After two solo flights, Vic started his acrobatic training. He did loops, barrel rolls, quick reversals and quick stops. They used retro rockets for the quick stops, but the quick reversal was an interesting maneuver. You just set your engines to idle, reversed the direction of your spacecraft, and then put the power back on. It stopped you as soon as possible and got you going the opposite direction as soon as possible. The ship had a mechanism for dealing with the G forces, he found. Normally a quick stop wouldn't be practical. Negative G forces are very detrimental to a human body. They cause "red out" which is much worse than "black out." After going through "red out" you generally have two black eyes and a splitting headache that will last for a day or two. But the ship used its gravity compensation mechanism to keep the quick stop from being uncomfortable.

Then after that was instrument training. He had already gone through it in the simulators. For flying in space instruments were all you had so you had to be proficient at instrument flying.

He was back to flying with an instructor for about half a dozen flights or so until he mastered all the details of instrument flying. Then they left the planet's atmosphere so he could get some practice flying out in space.

Next came formation flying. He found that Dan was ready to start his formation flying, too. Dan turned out to be his wingman.

"So we're gonna fly together now," said Vic as they left the ready room.

"Looks like it," answered Dan.

"So you'll get to see all my mistakes."

"Yeah, if you make any. I'm sure I'll make plenty."

At first they just learned to fly in pairs. So he and Dan practiced flying each other's wing. Naturally they each had an instructor riding in each spacecraft at first. They flew out over the Big Lake and practiced changing the lead. They learned to maintain a tight parade position if they were flying for show and a loose trail formation if they wanted more maneuverability. Then when their instructors determined they were ready they were permitted a couple of solo flights together.

They took off on a bright sunshiny day and flew to Big Lake. They noticed there were islands periodically along the lake. On one island they saw a couple of gals sunbathing. But they didn't dare fly low enough to get a close look. Regulations forbid them to fly below 1500 feet. He and Dan got to be good friends. Dan was a pleasant guy to be around.

After a couple of solo flights, they were back to flying with their instructors, learning formation acrobatics. Loops, barrel rolls, quick reversals, quick stops, and the same maneuvers they had learned before. They just did them in formation, now. Within a couple more weeks they were ready for some mock combat flights. Simulated dog fights.

Vic's first simulated dog fight was with Dan, of course, since Dan and Vic flew together. Off they flew on out of the atmosphere into the black of outer space. There was one benefit with outer space. You didn't have to deal with G forces at all if you were outside the gravitational field of any planet. And it was minimal even if you were within the gravitational field of a planet when you were above the atmosphere, because it would be such a light force.

Dan and Vic flew out in formation with an instructor flying chase. As soon as the instructor gave them three beeps on the radio as a signal to start, Vic immediately did a quick stop and changed course just enough to put Dan in his sights and pushed the kill button. The kill button was rigged to record a simulated kill and send it to the chase pilot's computer with a corresponding display on his instruments.

So the mock battle hadn't been in progress for more than two seconds before Vic had scored a kill. "Take it easy, Caveman 2. Your partner hasn't had any combat training before," he said to Vic.

Vic had a mischievous grin on his face as he keyed the mike and said, "Yes, sir." Then he turned away from him like as if to give him a shot and then did a quick stop, turned and had Dan right in his sights again. He scored another kill. Then he decided he'd have to just deliberately let Dan get him in his sights before he'd get in position to shoot. So he let Dan have a kill, then he got two more. But he still got about four kills to every one that Dan got. Dan did get some practice out of it. You have to start somewhere if you're going to learn.

On Vic's next flight they had him up against a different pilot, one he didn't know. But he beat him just as badly as he did Dan the previous day. Then he found out that two on one was part of their training and they decided to move Vic up to that level without further ado. Having to keep track of two "enemies" did make it more challenging for Vic but he made a good account of himself even then.

Vic had done well in his mock combat training in the Old Empire. He seemed to have a knack for it. He had been in only two actual space battles but didn't shoot anyone down. It was rare that a rookie pilot succeeded in scoring a kill in his first several space battles. To just survive the battle was generally a major accomplishment. But it was also because he didn't want to shoot down any of the Rebel pilots. So he either didn't get in firing position or deliberately fired to miss. He didn't want Rebel blood on his hands. He had the idea that he'd change sides when the opportunity arose when he first joined the Imperial Fleet. In fact, at that time, he had already been making plans to do so.

At the end of the week Vic had made a pretty good name for himself as a fighter pilot. All his instructors were impressed, even

Lieutenant Davis.

CHAPTER 11
FLEET MARINES

While Vic was doing his training flights in Seaside, Lieutenant Ben Scott was busy training his platoon in the mountains nearby. Lieutenant Scott was a platoon commander for the Fleet Marines. His platoon was a member of a crack regiment of mountain troops who were also trained paratroopers. In fact, para-jumping over mountainous terrain was their specialty. And hand to hand combat. And scaling sheer cliffs. For now he was busy training his platoon on a survival exercise. They were allowed no rations or water other than what they found in nature for their two month training exercise. They were allowed only their survival knives or hunting knives. And salt. They had to find their water and food in the wilderness environment they were training in.

This was no problem for Ben. He grew up in the mountains of Armenia. The mountains of Armenia were thick with rebel guerrilla soldiers. No one liked the Old Empire and fought against it if they ever had a chance. Ben's father had been a career poacher, both as a hunter and trapper. Ben remembered his coal black beard that matched his black hair. Ben's mother had been raped and killed by Imperial soldiers when they overran the village where they lived when he was three years old. He watched his father take on five regular soldiers single handed, kill them all with his hunting knife, then finding his young son still unharmed, scooped him up in his arms and escaped. That was where young Ben grew up, living off the land and surviving in the rugged mountains. His father traded furs and skins for what he needed on the black market. The cold winters were tough, but his father knew how to survive in the mountains. He'd always build a cabin somewhere in a protected place during the summer and make sure it was well stocked with fire wood and jerked meat by the time winter set in. Then after the first freeze, he'd build up his larder with fresh meat. So they had fresh meat during the first half of the winter and would save the jerky until the last several winter months when they would have starved without it.

They normally never wintered in the same spot two winters in a row for two reasons. One, when you trapped an area all winter, you'd normally find pickings would be much thinner the following year. But another reason was that it's better not to establish a permanent home. Not if you are a guerrilla soldier. You have to move often.

When Ben was thirteen he was a highly skilled guerilla soldier himself, in fact he had a least a dozen enemy soldiers to his credit by then. When he was fifteen, his father was captured and hanged. The grief of losing his mother was the biggest loss he had ever had in his life before that. He didn't see how he could keep living after he buried his father. He shed no tears. He was below grief.

But there is a big advantage to youth. You spring back fast. And for young Ben, to spring back meant to find a way to repay the ruthless Imperial Army for their crimes.

In selling furs, Ben's father had frequently dealt with smugglers. And Ben got to know them, too, of course. So he went to the cache where his father had stored their furs from the previous season. He loaded them into a canoe and started a trip to the rendezvous point. Then he made camp nearby where he could watch. When he saw the traders arrive he came up to them, cautiously as always and let them know he had some furs to trade.

Except, instead of money or supplies, he explained what he wanted in exchange for his furs was passage to the planet Ultaria. Olaf, the grizzled looking old smuggler, heard him explain about his father's death and how he wanted to join up with the Rebel forces. He was touched by the boy's story.

The carefully guarded secret to the location of Ultaria *was* known to smugglers. So the smuggler's ship landed him near the Dizzy Mountains on Ultaria and he made his way to Seaside and just walked into the recruiting station and said he wanted to join the Fleet Marines. That was five years ago. Now at age twenty, he had his own platoon, and was sharing with them his knowledge of survival and guerilla tactics to shape them up into the finest fighting force in the New Empire.

The survival knives they were issued wouldn't take an edge or hold an edge. There was a pocket attached to the knife sheaf to hold a whet stone but it didn't do you much good if the knife wouldn't take an edge to begin with. So most of the marines just brought their own knives. You could find knives made out of good steel in sporting supplies stores. And they were allowed to carry in their pockets whatever they would normally carry in combat so they each had a good pocket knife made from good steel. So they got by.

PFC Edgeworth had used his pocket knife to whittle out a sling shot stock from a piece of forked tree limb, as did Private Songson. They used rubber surgical tubing for the sling. It was something that they'd have in their survival pack while in combat so it was permissible.

Edgeworth had seen a rabbit and shot a piece of rock at it. Songson apparently saw the same rabbit and shot at it at the same time. The rabbit did keel over.

"Wow, I got him!" exclaimed Songson.

"No, you didn't!" Edgeworth replied. "I got him."

"I saw my rock hit him," insisted Songson.

Ben saw what was going on and said, "I don't care who shot the rabbit. We'll still have the meat and we'll have to share it anyway. Whoever shot it has to clean it, though."

"It's your rabbit," Songson decided quickly.

"No, I'm sure your rock is the one that killed it," Edgeworth said.

"You clean it," Ben said, gesturing toward Songson. "And you skin it," he said to Edgeworth.

That seemed to settle the dispute for the moment. The men had been catching things like snakes and lizards all afternoon. One of the marines had cleaned all the bark off of a long slender piece of tree limb and sharpened one end. Another marine started a fire. By skewering all the critters caught on that one stick they got them to cooking over the fire. With rabbits or squirrels, they quartered them first and skewered the quarters.

They had found a stream to camp near so they had water. But it was awkward to have to lay down and put your mouth in the stream to get a drink. It was good water, though. So they settled for a dinner with skimpy rations.

It was dark by the time they finished dinner so they decided to turn in. They had thin blankets made out of some kind of synthetic material that would fold up so it would fit in your pocket. Every survival pack had them. So the men wrapped themselves up in their thin blankets and went to sleep. They were able to sleep warm.

The next morning when they rose it was cold, of course, like it will be in the mountains even in summer. One of the men started a fire and two other men did likewise. Marines were huddled over all three fires to get warm.

"We have to make it to a checkpoint today," Ben told them.

"Yeah," Edgeworth said. They knew that the marines couldn't keep it simple. You not only had to figure out a way to get food and water but there were certain checkpoints they had to make every day or two. The marines thought it complicated things unnecessarily but orders were orders.

"You see that cliff over there?" Ben pointed to the east. "We're going to climb it." The marines turned around and looked.

"We can't climb that. That would be a technical climb," Songson said.

"It looks like a sheer cliff from here but there are places on the sides where it can be climbed," Ben replied.

"Brackett, you and Barnes are going to head out first as scouts. You'll climb it and when you reach the top you'll signal to us that all is clear and we'll make our climb."

This was similar to how they'd do it if in combat, so that made sense.

Brackett and Barnes started out and the men were put to either gathering wild berries or finding firewood for the fires. Since they had no axes, they could only gather up pieces of limbs lying on the ground and break them up. But they hadn't had breakfast, yet, and it gave them something to do.

After about a half an hour had passed, about a dozen or so marines walked up to the fire with their hats full of mountain berries. Ben had the corporals divide them up among the men and they had breakfast, such as it was. He had three corporals in the platoon, each was a squad leader.

It was about 0950 when Ben saw Brackett standing on top of the cliff waving at them. So he formed up the marines and started them down the small mountain they were on, heading across a draw toward the cliff.

Ben had briefed the men to look for prickly pear cactus while walking along. The root was very similar to potatoes. So they stopped frequently to take their survival knives and dig up the cactus roots. It was a little tricky cutting off the roots without getting pricked with the cactus needles. But they rubbed the dirt off the roots and put them in their pockets. The front pockets of their fatigues were large and would hold a lot.

When they reached the cliff Ben divided up the platoon into squads. Squad A took a trail up the peak to the left and squads B & C went up a trail to the right. The climbing was steep with lots of switchbacks and rocks but they were able to manage it. It was more difficult when done on limited rations. Ben himself noticed that he got tired much quicker than usual.

Ben took the point for Squad A. He did this sometimes so no one thought it unusual. When he reached the top he greeted Brackett and Barnes. He told them he was going to look around. He also told them to get started building four campfires. He didn't tell them why. He walked slowly and quietly through the woods. He spotted a spiked buck grazing. He was downwind from the buck and continued to walk slowly, keeping trees between himself and the buck as much as possible. He got within 25 or 30 yards. Then he took out his survival knife and threw it underhand. The knife struck the buck just behind the shoulder. His knife had an 8 inch blade and was sharp as a razor. The buck ran maybe 30 yards before it fell over. Ben waited to give it time to bleed and get weaker before he approached it. Then he walked up to it, pulled out the knife and field dressed it. Then he started dragging it toward camp. He knew that the men weren't good enough in the woods to get that close to a deer without being seen. But he knew he could.

When he arrived back in camp all the marines had completed their climb to the top and had four big campfires going. Ben assigned two men to skin out the deer. Then he quartered it and when the marines saw what he was doing four of them started whittling out spits to go over the fire. Soon they had four quarters of meat on four different spits roasting over the fires.

So on their second night out every marine in the platoon ate all the red meat he wanted. They decided they liked being in Lieutenant Scott's platoon.

As for as Ben was concerned, he wanted the men well fed. They got along with each other better and had more endurance.

CHAPTER 12
BRAWLING

The war games and military exercises in the mountains normally would last from two weeks to two months. This particular survival training exercise was a two month exercise. So after two months he brought his platoon back to the base. He turned in his report to his company commander. Then he cleaned up and went over to the officer's club. He normally would go to the Fleet Marine Officer's club, have a few drinks and get intoxicated and shine up to one of the women that frequented the Club.

But sometimes for a change, he'd go over to the Fleet Officer's club. So after he'd brought his platoon back to the base at the end of their survival training, he got a shower and shave, changed into a clean uniform and headed over to the Fleet club. He walked into the bar and to the middle of the room, pulled out a chair from an empty table, climbed up and stood on it and said, "Anyone here wanna fight?"

All the Fleet officers looked up with an amused look on their faces. So Ben was here. Most of them were used to him and were merely entertained by his antics. No one answered. Standing on the chair, Ben turned around in a complete circle like as if to find a willing taker. Everyone looked at him with a half smile but no one said anything. Then he said, "Well, neither do I. Let me buy all of you a drink," and he climbed down from the chair and headed for the bar. He had two months' back pay in his pocket.

Vic and Dan had just got in from a training flight. They had decided to drop by the club for a drink before going home. Vic hadn't seen Ben before. A Fleet Marine. What do you expect? All of them were a little crazy.

Then Ben took his drink and walked over toward a table where three young ladies were sitting. He didn't sit down. He stood in front of them and said, "Hello ladies. I hate to see three such beautiful ladies drinking alone." All three of them blushed beautifully.

"I climb mountains and I gaze at all the beautiful trees and mountain peaks and the sky and clouds, but nowhere, ever, have I ever seen anything as beautiful as you three." They were all three smiling, at first tolerantly. But they obviously enjoyed being entertained. He was laying it on thick. "But I also drink and gamble. And I lie a lot. And I get in fights. In fact, I guess you could say I have nothing but faults. In fact I probably have more faults and sins to my credit than anyone else here."

Ben was a very handsome lad and his manner was one of abject innocence in spite of his loud mouth manner. But the girls found him entertaining and were perfectly willing to listen to him.

Then a big burly ship's officer came stomping toward him. "You leave those women alone!" he snarled. He was trying to get something going with the blonde gal. He had made no headway, yet. Of course Ben knew nothing about his fruitless endeavors. He just calmly waited until he came up and when he swung a right he simply side stepped, gave him a kidney punch, turned him around and kicked him vigorously in the tail bone and then turned back to the three ladies he was entertaining. Five more junior officers from his ship came over since they decided their friend needed some help. Vic and Dan saw what was developing and they didn't see any harm the marine lieutenant was doing. And they both had a keen sense of fair play so they hurried over to see what help they could give Ben. Ben had all five of them lying on the floor before they could get across the room. Then he came to meet them and grabbed them both and half carried them back to the bar they'd just come from and told the bartender, "I'd like to buy both these gentleman a drink."

The base police had arrived by then. They found the six brawlers lying on the floor. They handcuffed them and escorted them out. Ben just calmly paid for the drinks he had ordered. Then he turned around and stood between Vic and Dan and sipped his drink and watched the brawlers being removed from the room just like any innocent bystander would do.

* * *

Ben introduced himself to Vic and Dan. After they'd drained their glasses, Dan grabbed the bar dice and rolled the dice to see who bought the next drink. Vic excused himself because he knew that Red was waiting for him. He didn't want to be inconsiderate of her.

"Why go elsewhere? There's three women right over there. One for each of us," Ben suggested. "Will she give you 3 days on bread and water if you're late?"

"I promised a lady I'd go by as soon as I got off duty. I just figured I'd do what I said I'd do." It looked like he was going to be a wet blanket. But Vic was very independent about such things. He left.

The following Friday night, Vic had Red meet him at the officer's club when she got off work and she had a few drinks with him. Dan was there.

When Red walked in, Vic stepped away from the bar to greet her. He gave her a kiss and a hug, oblivious of their audience. Then he turned and said, "This is my flying partner, Dan. Dan, this is Red."

"Why hello, Dan," she smiled up at him and offered him her hand.

Dan found himself overcome by her charm as was the case for any man. He now understood why Vic gave her the priority that he did. He'd be eager to get home, too, if he had a woman this beautiful.

The bartender came up and Red ordered a glass of wine. She didn't want to get tipsy with this many men around. But she was glad that Vic had asked her to come in. It was good to meet his friends. Then Ben Scott walked in. As soon as he saw him, Vic waved and said, "Hello Ben. Over here."

Ben came walking over. He ordered a bottle of Old Red. Vic introduced him to Red. He bowed low when she offered him her hand and he kissed it lightly. "At your service ma'am," he said. Oh, Ben could be a gentleman when he wanted to. It was just that he could also be a ruffian if that was what he wanted. And if he decided to be a ruffian, you could be sure he'd be a good one.

After a couple of drinks they were starting to feel hungry. "You two are welcome to join us, if you like," Vic told them as he took

Red's hand to lead her to a table. Vic went to a table big enough for four people.

"Good idea," Ben said as he followed them. "But," he said, "let's sit at this table." He had chosen a round table that was big enough for six people. As soon as Vic, Red and Dan sat down, Ben excused himself. In 5 minutes he was back with two beautiful young women, a blonde for himself and a brunette for Dan. He introduced the blonde to them, Kim was her name. And then he introduced them to the brunette whose name was Jean.

Vic and Dan both stood up. Ben held out the chair for the blonde first and got her seated, then did the same for Jean.

"So you men are from the Fleet," Kim ventured.

"Fleet pilots," Vic said and pointed to himself and Dan. "And even worse, a Fleet Marine," he said when he gestured to Ben. Ben swelled at the compliment.

They learned that Kim and Jean were both base employees. They worked in the Administrative office. They liked to go to the club on Friday nights before going home. They were roommates and shared an apartment just off the base.

After they ordered another round of drinks a dinner waiter came by and they ordered something to eat. Some kind of sea food and potatoes, Vic found out they were called on this planet. And they each ordered another bottle of Old Red.

After dinner a band started playing and Vic got up, excused himself and Red and led her to the dance floor. Within a couple of minutes, Vic saw Ben and Dan on the dance floor with Kim and Jean.

Red had been to the officer's club before, of course, many times, in fact. Being the daughter of an Admiral meant she grew up on a military base. And she knew some of the men, there. But this was the first time she'd been here with Vic. And it was fun. Vic could tell by looking at her that she was having a good time. He was glad he asked her to come and meet him here.

* * *

Ben didn't come by the officer's club every Friday night. He was frequently on the mountain with his men. But when he did come back down from the mountain he'd always be thirsty. And he started coming to the Fleet Officer's Club more often. He didn't have any problem finding a beautiful lady to join him. Then he'd bring her over and introduce her to Vic and Dan. Any time he saw Dan sitting alone, he'd bring over two women, as before. They'd always find a table big enough for six people if Vic and Red were along and have dinner and a small party.

The band generally started playing at 9 o'clock and they'd normally dance the rest of the evening.

CHAPTER 13
SUNDAY PICNIC

Vic had every Sunday off. He was on duty from 7 AM until 9:30 PM every Monday through Friday while he was still doing his simulator training. Simulator training was always in the evenings. His simulator training continued after he started his training flights though he now got Friday nights off. The simulator was especially useful for learning emergency procedures and such. Emergencies didn't happen very often in flight and it wasn't always feasible to simulate an emergency while flying. So they used the simulator for that purpose.

But he had Friday nights and Saturday nights off. He got off early enough on Saturday night to take Red out on the town. And he had finally got a payday. He had drawn an advance on his pay when he first picked up his orders so he wasn't completely broke. But now he decided he had enough money to rent an air car and take Red to an island that he had flown over several times out in the middle of Big Lake.

They left Red's apartment at about 8 AM and loaded up their stuff into the rental air car. Then they took off and headed toward the Dizzy Mountains. He had made sure he got a car with the capability of sufficient altitude to fly over the mountains. Their highest peaks went up to 15,000 feet or thereabouts. So off they went into the wild blue yonder. Once they were past the mountains they noticed the beautiful deep blue of the water of the lake. It was an especially beautiful day and the water was completely calm. They saw an occasional fishing boat as they flew out over the lake. Vic headed for the island that he had picked out. He had picked out a small island with no inhabitants. He landed the air car and they got out and unloaded their gear and set up their picnic chairs and unfolded a picnic table. Red then pulled off her top and Vic noticed she had on a skimpy bikini, white with red stripes. She looked really good. In fact, he noted that she had a terrific figure. He pulled off his clothes, too. He had a swimming suit on under them. They waded out into the water to get out where it was deep enough to swim. And the water was *cold.* But they adjusted to it quickly. After swimming vigorously for a few minutes they were ready to come back in. They got in to the point where it was too shallow to swim and waded the rest of the way in. They had brought two surf boards but the water was too calm for surfing.

They barbequed steaks at noon time and had some potato salad that Red had brought along and some bottles of Old Red. Red explained where most of the red meat came from that was consumed in Oceanside. She told Vic that the mountains just to the east of Oceanside had herds of deer and mountain sheep. Professional hunters hunted them and sold the meat and hides to the meat and leather markets in Oceanside. The hunters had to be licensed and there was a limit to the number of licenses issued each year. Each hunter had a limit but also had a quota, too. The quota was necessary to maintain the herds at the proper number. There was no facility for grazing animals on the continent so all the red meat came from the mountains. There were other continents on the planet with grazing lands and also farms to produce grain to fatten meat animals. But the majority of the red meat consumed in Oceanside came from the mountains.

Red explained also that all the water for Oceanside and Lakeside both came from mountain streams. Warm moist air from the ocean moved over Oceanside and would move up the mountains from the west. As it moved up the mountainsides it naturally cooled down to its dew point. So rain in the mountains was frequent. And rain on the east side of mountains, also. Rain was not so frequent in Oceanside.

And she explained that there was a hydroelectric plant in the middle of the mountain range powered by a large waterfall that provided both Oceanside and Lakeside with electrical power. The waterfall ran into Big Lake.

After they'd eaten they just sat in their lawn chairs and enjoyed the fresh air. Vic wanted Red to put on some sun screen because he didn't want her to get a sun burn on her beautiful body. She blushed but she did dope up with sun screen. Then she came over and started rubbing him with sun screen, too.

That afternoon the wind came up so they had waves. They got

their surfboards out and started surfing. Vic took a spill and hit the water with a splash. Red couldn't help but laugh. Vic ignored her. He got on his surf board and got going again and Red took a spill. Vic laughed and when Red's head popped up out of the water and she saw him laughing, she stuck her tongue out at him. They kept on surfing until they were tired.

When it was finally time to load up and head back to the city, they were exhausted. Exhausted but happy. When they got back to Red's apartment, she fixed them some dinner. Vic started to leave and she walked to the door and clung to him. Vic held her and squeezed her. But she didn't let go. Vic felt his entire body engulfed in a warm feeling. But he thought he should be going. It was getting late. He tried to pull loose from her and she said, "Please don't leave me alone!" with a pleading tone to her voice. So Vic spent the night in her apartment. She explained that she couldn't stand to be alone after being with such good company all day. He felt the same way.

Once Vic's simulator training was over with, he no longer had to work in the evenings. He got off at 6 PM every day. So he just started the practice of going over to Red's apartment every night when he got off duty and they would sometimes eat out and sometimes dine in, but he didn't bother to go back to the barracks. He'd leave to go on duty from her apartment every morning. Vic started buying the groceries since Red did almost all the cooking. She explained that she liked to cook. So he figured he should pay for all the groceries then, to keep things fair. Sometimes they would barbeque steaks on the roof of her apartment and then play music and sing. She played a wind corder and Vic played a uke harp. But he also took her dancing at least once a week.

CHAPTER 14
PLANETARY PATROL

Vic now had a pair of space wings fastened to the chest of his flight suit. He took his fighter craft on out to the limit of his patrol. Then he started his turn. His mission was simply to fly a race track pattern in his patrol sector and keep his sensors tuned in to pick up the presence of any unknown spacecraft in the area. He had completed his transition training the previous week and he was now certified in the Fleet spacecraft fighter he was flying. His job was similar to what it had been while in the Imperial Fleet. He was spaceborne about ten hours each day. He only had to spend about an hour or so flying to his patrol sector and an hour on the return trip. He was on station for eight hours. About two hours were spent each day on briefing and flight planning. So he had to work a twelve hour day in all.

Boring work. But he knew how easy it is to get more excitement than you wanted in a very short period of time so he monitored his instruments carefully. He just flew out to the limit of the solar system in his sector and then turned around and flew back. At the end of his 8 hour patrol a relief spacecraft would arrive.

Fighter craft were used for scouting missions and patrol missions because they needed the maneuverability of a fighter craft. But if a lone spacecraft was attacked by a major force it would almost surely be shot down after hopefully getting a radio message off to Scout Control first so a scramble could be done to meet the enemy force. Vic knew that the location of Ultaria was a carefully guarded secret but what if her location was compromised? He had found Ultaria. So how could he be sure others wouldn't do so, too? He was not aware that smuggling ships sometimes landed on Ultaria. But for now he just flew his patrol sector and did his best to endure the boredom.

Then Vic felt a shudder and his cockpit lights went out. He was in total darkness! What is this? he thought. His emergency lighting system flicked on in a couple of seconds so he could see his instruments. His engine was losing power. Now this isn't good, he thought! Within a few minutes his engine went down to idle speed and then quit running completely. He attempted a re-start and after the third try his engine started running again. But if it went out once, it could go out again. And he found out he couldn't reach full power. He managed to get it up to half power but that was as high as it would go.

"Scout Control, Scout Control, This is Watchdog 8," he said over the radio. He figured he'd better get his distress call in now while he still had battery power. With no electrical power at all he wouldn't even have a radio.

There was no answer on the radio at first but he tried calling them again and this time they answered. "Go ahead Watchdog 8."

"I had an engine failure momentarily. I succeeded in getting it re-started but it's only capable of running at half power."

"Roger, Watchdog 8, Standby," was Scout Patrol's answer.

After a few minutes he heard the message over his earphones, "Watchdog 8, this is Scout Control."

Vic keyed the mike and said, "This is Watchdog 8, go ahead."

"Your instructions are to continue on your patrol. Your relief is en route to your position. A tug will be dispatched to pull your spacecraft in if your engine fails again."

"This is Watchdog 8. Thanks. Out," Vic answered. Maybe his engine would stay on the line now. You really didn't need much power in outer space. There was no air drag to overcome. But you had to have power to maneuver against the gravitational pull of any planet nearby. And he couldn't land on a dead engine. Without reverse thrust his spacecraft would turn into a fireball as soon as he entered the atmosphere of the planet.

In another hour or so, Vic saw his relief on his EWD (Early Warning Detection) screen. He identified it as a friendly. When it was on station, he heard the radio message, "Ready to relieve you, Watch Dog 8."

"Good," he answered. "No activity."

"Roger," the other pilot answered.

Vic headed back to the home planet. His engine kept running but he found that he still couldn't exceed half power. Half power was enough to get her in and maneuver to a landing. He did meet the tug before he got to the home planet and it escorted him down. He set her down and went through his secure checklist. After he left the spacecraft he had to attend a debriefing in the ready room. But the debriefing didn't take more than five minutes if they had nothing unusual to report. Then he had to go to the maintenance department and fill out a report for the maintenance personnel so they would have a few clues at the front end to trouble shoot the problem with the engine.

Then he went to the locker room and changed from his flight suit to his uniform and headed over to Red's apartment. She met him at the door with a hug. She had dinner ready.

He sat down to eat. "How did your day go?" she asked, after she was seated, too.

"Fine," he replied. "I'm worn out. Twelve hours a day does get me tired. But I don't mind being tired when I get to be with you," and he looked over at her. She blushed slightly. It apparently didn't take much to make her blush. He didn't mention his engine failure. He didn't see any reason to worry her unnecessarily.

"I enjoy being with you, too," she said in reply. "Anything exciting happen on your patrol?"

"No. Just boredom all day long. But there's things worse than boredom can happen to a man." He obviously was a died in the wool Fleet officer, she thought. Even boredom is okay. But Vic knew that the life of a Fleet spacecraft pilot was made up of hours and hours of boredom interrupted with moments of stark terror. Boredom was better than terror when you compared the two.

But Red sensed that he was withholding something. She looked at him and with a look of distress on her face said, "What happened out there?" Vic learned very quickly that he couldn't lie to her after all. She was too alert to his feelings for him to keep it a secret from her.

"My engine did conk out momentarily but I succeeded in getting it restarted." He now knew that telling her the truth was his only option.

"Your engine conked out? And what if you had failed to get it restarted?"

"Then scout control would have dispatched a tug out to tow me into the spaceport. As it was, they sent out a tug anyway to escort me in." The solution was so simple and sensible. Red calmed down when he told her that. So he wasn't really in much danger after all.

Vic was the only man Red had ever known who wouldn't lie to her. And that was one thing very important to her. Did he lie to her when he said everything went fine? No, everything did go fine, so it wasn't a lie but he was going to withhold the truth if she hadn't pressed the issue. But she pressed the issue. She didn't have the "power" like her father had but she could still usually tell if someone was lying to her by the look in their eyes and their facial expressions.

* * *

The next morning Vic was up at 0400. He got dressed and left without waking Red. He got breakfast on the base. He had to brief at 0500. After breakfast he went to the locker room and changed into his flight suit. He had to be spaceborne by 0700 so he could be on station by 0800.

CHAPTER 15
URBAN WARFARE

When they weren't training in mountain warfare, the Fleet Marines would train in urban warfare. Lieutenant Ben Scott started putting two and two together. There apparently was some kind of campaign in the planning phase that was going to require mountain operations and urban operations, because all their training exercises were in those two categories. And para-jumping.

It wasn't practical to conduct training exercises in the city, itself, of course. They had a place out in the desert on the east side of the mountains and north of the Big Lake where a mocked up town had been put together out of plywood. It was pretty realistic. Each house had four walls and some of them several rooms, so the marines could practice taking each house, one at a time.

And they had a sniper's roost mounted on a tower that resembled a church steeple on a building with several floors. So his men could practice flushing out snipers.

Ben had his platoon about 5 miles from the town on the east. His men had to approach the town running, zigzagging, then when a mock laser burst hit among them, hit the dirt. Then after a few minutes they had to get up and run again. They ran the entire 5 miles, with their only rest being diving for the dirt, waiting a few minutes and then getting up again. When they were within a hundred yards or so of the "town" Ben heard the order from the company commander shouting into a mega horn, "Full speed!" At which time the platoon went into a sprint.

Ben was in good shape but they were required to run the five miles at a good clip. So he concluded he wasn't in *that* good a shape, after all. But after he got his second wind he was able to take his attention off of his fatigue and focus it on his men. He had to run in front since he was the platoon leader. And his platoon sergeant had to bring up the rear. But the physical exertion crowded out any feelings of anxiety that he would normally have felt. That was good, at least.

After the hundred yard sprint, they arrived at the first line of buildings. Ben was still breathing heavily and he could hear the men behind. Their heavy breathing sounded like there was a steam engine following him. But he saw little spots of light flashing up periodically in various places. It was to simulate laser fire. It was simulated simply by low intensity laser flashes. Referees were located at strategic points to score any simulated kills. It was a very complicated game. And exhausting. But the regimental commander wanted his men in top shape. And so did Ben for that matter. The one way to minimize your losses in any battle was to have the marines in tip top shape.

Ben let his men catch their breath for a few minutes after he got them in position. That's something they might not have time for in combat. But he knew he had to get them in shape in phases. They were especially winded from their last little sprint. Simulated losses resulted in probably a dozen of his men being tagged as hit. So they had to get up and walk off. They were temporarily out of the exercise at that point. They'd rejoin later so they'd get their share of training.

Then Ben told Sergeant Rohr to take Squad "A" down the street over on their left. Then he turned to Corporal Jones, "And you take the one to the right with Squad 'C'.

Corporal West, you take Squad 'B' down the middle street." He always had the squad leader take the point on the initial phases of any training operation. He reasoned that a squad leader couldn't very well train other men to do something he hadn't done himself enough times to have it really down. Later the squad leader would rotate the point position so that each man in each squad got his turn. He took his turn at taking the point, too, for that same reason.

As soon as the other two squads were in position he raised his arm and signaled them to go. All three squads started at once. When Corporal West started his squad, Ben waited until all the men were gone and he followed after. This way he could observe how the entire platoon performed. There would be a debriefing at the end of the exercise and the referees would tell them how they did.

Sergeant Ruhr took the first "house." He went up to the door, kicked it in, jumped to the side and threw inside a fire cracker which simulated a grenade. Then he jumped into the doorway with his blast rifle. There were several dummies on the floor that simulated enemy soldiers. He put a burst into each dummy with his blast rifle.

The other members of the squad were doing the same with the other houses on the block. It took maybe five minutes to take one block of city.

By noon they were exhausted and covered with dirt. But they had "taken" the city. Ben dispatched the platoon to various locations to guard the entrances to the city, then called the head referee on the radio, in this case Major Bandley, and reported the town secure. Major Bandley acknowledged his report and told him he could secure his platoon from the exercise.

So Ben had his men gather on the outskirts of the city and they built a campfire so they could heat up their field rations. They each had a package of dehydrated rations. All they had to do was open the can, pour in a little water and then heat it up with a pair of tongs furnished in their packs. It made a kind of stew and was pretty palatable. It fact, it tasted delicious as hungry as they were. And they had a metal cup that they'd hold over the fire with their tongs and heat water to make tea.

After lunch, Major Bandley met with Ben and debriefed him. His men did well, but he was told he should have moved into the town as soon as he reached the outskirts instead of letting the men rest. Major Bandley was a slave driver. So Ben wasn't surprised.

After that his men had to make a march across the desert. Twelve miles. Then they arrived at a creek where they'd camp. They certainly got plenty of physical conditioning with these exercises. His men should be in shape by the time they had to go into combat.

CHAPTER 16
FORMALITIES

Vic had a rotating shift. He worked the day shift for a month and then shifted over to the night shift for a month. Then he'd change back to a day shift for a month. He also went straight to Red's apartment when he got off duty. He was a little concerned at first about living with the admiral's daughter. He mentioned this to Red.

"Trial marriages are socially acceptable on Ultaria," she explained.

"It there something we have to do to make it a trial marriage?" he asked.

"Yes, we have a formal dinner in which we announce that we have started a trial marriage."

So he asked Red if she would make the arrangements to have a formal dinner to initiate a trial marriage and she agreed. He figured since she was the admiral's daughter that she'd know all the specifics of protocol. That was something in which he didn't have confidence. After all, he did come from a different planet.

In the meantime, Vic moved all of his gear from the barracks on base to her apartment. He didn't have much, just his uniforms and shaving kit. Then a week later, she explained that she had set a date for their formal dinner. It would be on a Saturday night. And she briefed him on what he'd have to wear. He'd have to wear his dinner dress uniform with black tie and tails.

Back to duty. Flying patrols. Boring. But he knew how important it was to keep the planet well protected. And his fighter craft was fully armed. He could shoot down an intruder with his laser guns very efficiently.

Finally, the day arrived for the formal dinner. And he was a little nervous while getting dressed. He had had to purchase a dinner dress uniform. He didn't already have one. The dinner dress uniform wasn't part of their standard uniform issue. Red insisted that he have it fitted so it would fit perfectly. Red wore a beautiful light blue gown. Bare shoulders, enough dip to her neckline to show some beautiful cleavage. She had done her hair up on top of her head so that it looked simply stunning. She was beautiful all over. But she was always beautiful all over no matter what she did. It was just more so tonight.

After getting dressed they went out to get a ground taxi to find that the admiral had sent his air car with an official driver for them. The driver was holding the door open. They climbed in and the driver drove them to the dinner hall.

They joined the reception line. Red pushed Vic to the head of the line. Vic found out that in the reception line was also Dan and Ben, friends of the groom to be. Then three women that Vic didn't know. They were Red's cousins, he learned, and he was introduced to them. He didn't see the Admiral but he knew he'd be there.

After they had completed the reception line, one woman walked up to them. She looked kind of middle aged. She had on a formal with bare shoulders but not showing any breast. She didn't have any breast to show was probably the reason. She had black hair and a kind of irritable look on her face.

"So this is the Imperial pilot you came up with," she said in a rather haughty manner.

"Jealous?" said Red with a haughty expression on her face as well. Vic had never seen her look that way before.

"Glad to meet you ma'm," he said trying to retain his polite demeanor.

"I'm not glad to meet you," she said angrily. "I was hoping the Admiral's daughter could find something better than a turncoat!"

"Move off," commanded Red. The woman glared at Vic a minute and then moved off.

Red grabbed Vic by the arm and led him over to a table and had him sit down. "Don't mind what she says. She's not well liked by anyone."

"I can understand that," said Vic. "In fact, I wonder how she got invited here."

"She's the wife of one of the admirals. That's why she was invited. But Daddy is the Commander in Chief of the Fleet. Her husband is junior to him. And she's junior to me."

"She's junior to you?" he sounded bewildered.

"I'm talking about social rank, not military rank. She's the wife of an admiral that's junior to my father. That makes her junior to me socially. Though what Daddy always taught me while I was growing up was that it wasn't really who you're married to or what family you grew up in that determines social rank. He said it's your value to society. Her name is Sandy and all she does is go to fancy balls and gossip and make snide remarks to people that do amount to something. So she doesn't do very much for society herself."

"Interesting," he said. It was obvious he was unperturbed.

"She didn't ruin your evening?"

"When I'm standing next to the most beautiful woman in the galaxy?" And she blushed just like he knew she would. And grabbed his hand and squeezed it.

"We need to go to the main table, now. It's getting to be time for dinner to be served," she told him.

So she led him to a long table in which couples were arranged on either side of it. Red showed Vic where he was supposed to sit. It was on the right side of the head of the table. And she sat on the left side opposite from him. Then they heard someone call "Please rise."

The Admiral came walking in, in his full dinner dress regalia. Six rows of medals on his chest as well as a pair of space pilot's wings. He went to the head of the table and sat down. Then everyone else took their seats.

Vic had noticed ever since they had arrived that Red had assumed a commanding presence. He'd never seen her that way before. And he continued to be further impressed with her as the evening progressed. She knew just what to do and made decisions quickly and easily. And she wasn't the slightest bit reluctant to tell Vic what to do. And he noticed that it didn't rub him wrong at all when she did. He was partly amused by seeing this side of her. And he didn't mind letting her have the lead when she was better qualified to do something than he. And she was definitely better qualified than he to handle things at a formal dinner such as this one.

Everyone was served before the Admiral. But no one touched their food. Then when the Admiral was served his food he immediately started eating which was everyone else's cue to do the same. A wine waiter came around pouring wine. Vic tasted the food. It was delicious. He tasted the wine. It was delicious. And he looked over at the red headed lady sitting across from him. She was beautiful. That was all he could say.

After they had finished eating, the Admiral stood up and gave them a speech. He told them about his "little girl" who was sitting beside him. He mainly described what a pleasure it was to raise her. She was Daddy's little girl from the first and while he knew he spoiled her rotten from the time she was born she never acted spoiled. She blushed when he said that. Then he beckoned to her to stand up. Then he beckoned Vic to do the same. He then introduced Vic to the group and explained that Vic was an excellent fighter pilot, and veteran of many battles and a fine officer. But what he appreciated most was the fact that his daughter was so much happier now than she was before she met him. Then he sat down. The waiters came back serving dessert.

Short and sweet, thought Vic. But what he did say seemed to be just what was appropriate. Vic decided he liked Fleet social life.

CHAPTER 17
FLYING SAUCER

Vic brought his flying saucer to a hover over Red's apartment complex. He picked out the landing pad reserved for her apartment and eased down toward it. He was especially careful as he brought it on down, because he hadn't landed this baby very many times, yet. He'd taken off and landed several times for practice at the dealership where he bought it.

Two months previously Vic found out that he was drawing extra hazardous duty pay now that he was flying missions for the Fleet. He decided his pay was sufficient to make the payments on a personal flying saucer. So he saved his money for a couple of months in order to make the down payment. Then he made a personal loan at a bank for the balance. Red's apartment, of course, had landing pads on the roof for ground cars and saucers. Vic's new aircraft was a small craft, barely room enough for two people in the cockpit but it was fine for his purposes. It had a luggage compartment that opened from the outside. He decided it would be cheaper than renting a ground car in the long run.

Vic walked down the steps and down the hall to Red's apartment. He stopped and knocked. She opened the door in a couple of seconds to greet him with a beautiful smile. She had on white short shorts and white sneakers. And her shorts were really short. She had on a red halter top that showed her navel and about four inches of skin below it. She had a white ribbon in her hair that matched her shorts and red sox that matched her halter top. She looked just beautiful from head to foot. She always looked beautiful. But each time he saw her he was overawed by her beauty all over again. She almost always dressed sexy when she was with Vic. And that was the only time that she dressed sexy normally.

Vic was dressed in knee length shorts and a T shirt. The shorts were khaki and the T shirt dark blue. He had on white sneakers and white sox. He helped her carry her stuff up to the roof. He opened the baggage compartment and stowed the picnic equipment and basket of food. Then he opened her door and showed her where to sit. Then he went around to his door and got in. He showed Red how to strap in, then strapped in himself. He went over his before start checklist, started up his drives, then did his before take-off check list. He moved the little ship smoothly off the roof and toward the Dizzy Mountains to their east.

When they crossed the mountains, Red was impressed with the view. The mountains were really huge and were covered with tall pine trees. And after they crossed the summit of the mountain range, she could see Big Lake. The deep blue of the lake going as far as she could see was impressive. As they flew across the lake they could see fishing boats periodically and occasionally an island or two.

When they reached the island Vic was looking for he brought his ship down and landed her on a public landing pad. This island was inhabited and had marinas and other things to attract tourists. He and Red walked over to the marina and looked at their boat rentals. Vic picked out the one he wanted and paid the marina attendant for a one day rental. He took it around and beached it near his new saucer. He and Red got out and went to the saucer. He unlocked the baggage compartment and got out his fishing gear and the picnic basket that Red had packed. Then they went back down to the beach, loaded everything into the boat and Vic hit the start button. The boat was powered by an electric motor, which in turn was powered by batteries that were charged by a solar power plant. He thought it was neat, the things that engineers came up with these days.

Vic got the boat moving, then pushed forward on the throttle to get her up on the plane. Then he headed out, looking for likely coves to see if he could find where the fish were hiding. He saw the head of a tributary over on the right coastline and headed for it. As he approached it, he slowed down the boat, then set it for troll. He picked up his pole and tossed out his line. Red watched what he was doing and did the same. He had a surface lure tied to the end of his line. So he reeled the slack out of the line, and then gave it a jerk. He reeled the slack out again and gave it another jerk. Red watched what he was doing and she did the same. On the third cast, Red's pole bent double.

"Reel it in. Hold your line tight," yelled Vic. He was as excited as she was. She reeled for all she was worth. Vic had set the drag for her pole for her. The reel started screaming as the fish swam away from them. Then the line went slack again. "Reel it in again, don't let your line go slack." Vic was calmer now. She did so.

It was a surprise to Vic that the fish didn't succeeded in spitting out the hook when the line went slack. But she followed Vic's instructions and didn't let the line go slack again. Finally she managed to reel the fish up near the boat. Vic grabbed the landing net and scooped up the fish. He flipped the rim of the net over to make it impossible for the fish to jump out and put it in the bottom of the boat.

"Honey, that must be at least an 8 pound fish. Looks like a lunker. And they're good to eat." She was finally starting to calm down from the excitement of her catch. And Vic didn't even know if she'd been fishing before.

"Have you been fishing before, Angel?" he asked.

She shook her head with the most innocent look on her face. Or naive might be a better word for it. Well, Vic wasn't complaining. The first fish she'd ever caught was a trophy lunker.

After the fish stopped fighting so much, Vic reached into the net and got it by the gills. He put it in the fish well that was full of water and closed the lid. He knew it wasn't dead because it's gills were still working.

"Well, we've got enough for a really good lunch even if we don't catch anything else." It had never occurred to fishermen on this continent to have a fish mounted. All sporting fish were also food fish. They were people with a very practical nature. This wasn't true of other continents. In Gorienth, trophy fishing was very popular. You could charter a boat with a fighting chair and catch fish weighing several hundred pounds sometimes. And it was customary to have a fish mounted to hang on the wall if it was of trophy size. But here, it was customary to take a photograph of a trophy fish but you didn't waste the fish since it was good to eat.

By noon Vic had caught 5 fish and Red had caught another two. But her 8 pounder was the biggest of the day so far. Vic pulled the boat in and beached her. They carried their fish to the cleaning pavilion and Vic filleted them out and put them on ice. They decided not to fish any more that day so Vic took the boat around to turn it back in while Red started cooking at the picnic cooking facility. When Vic got back he unfolded two lawn chairs. He sat down in one of them and watched a beautiful woman standing over the picnic stove turning fish and cooking some kind of vegetables. He had brought two quart bottles of Old Red and let her know that one of them was for her. She looked over her shoulder and smiled at him and said she'd be over in just a minute.

So they had fried fish, veggies and Old Red for lunch. And it hit the spot. About an hour or so after they had finished eating they decided to go swimming. They went to the flying saucer to change into their swim suits. Vic couldn't help but notice again how beautiful Red looked in her bikini. Red with yellow stripes on it this time.

After a couple of hours of swimming and splashing they decided they were tired. They loaded up their gear and headed back for home.

CHAPTER 18
SMUGGLER SHIP ARRIVES

The men and women were boarding the spacecraft. The group was made up mostly of people that had been in trouble with the law. Some of them were escaped political prisoners. Others were people the authorities were looking for to arrest. But they were all people that would rather fight than be slaves.

Nina was none of the above. Her parents had been killed helping prisoners escape. Since she was their daughter she was wanted by the law though she herself had committed no crime.

Nina's face was still beautiful in spite of her perpetual frown. Her hair was still beautiful in spite of being uncombed and unkempt. She had walked a quarter of a mile with two water bags, one on each shoulder to a brook to get water. The smugglers came and told the refugees it was time to board the ship. When Nina returned with her two full water bags everyone was gone.

In the meantime, the refugees had finished boarding the smuggler ship, the hatches were closed and the ship's crew prepared for takeoff. The drives were started. After they had warmed up, the ship floated up clear of the surface. Then it continued to float on up. Up, up, up, clear of the atmosphere of Armenia. Nina saw the large cargo ship rise above the trees and drift on up into the sky.

The passengers inside the ship had been camping out in the mountains for weeks. They were dirty and ragged. They were city folks and they considered the mountain streams were too cold to use for bathing. And their clothes weren't suitable for living in the mountains.

The leader of their group had escaped from prison and robbed a bank to finance their trip. Their destination was the planet Glotta where they were told they could find jobs. Glotta was a planet that welcomed refugees from the Empire. It was an under-populated planet that needed people.

After they were clear of the planet's atmosphere the captain gave the helmsman the course to fly to hopefully stay clear of the Imperial patrol craft. The officer of the deck reported that there were Imperial forces in the area. The captain immediately gave the helmsman a new course to evade detection. Too late. The enemy ships were heading for them. Space fighter craft by the way they maneuvered. They could see this on the detection gear screen.

The captain gave orders to the helmsman to change both course and speed every few seconds to make themselves a more difficult target. He had a tail laser but that was his only armament. He set a course to get as far away from the attacking forces as possible, but of course, the attackers were able to overtake them. When they were in range the captain gave the order to the tail gunner to start firing. The fighter craft easily outmaneuvered the laser blasts and kept coming. Two fighters were now showing on their detection gear.

When one of the laser blasts connected with the smuggler's ship, the captain knew it was all over. The first blast destroyed their protective shield and the blast from the second fighter disabled their engines. The laser gunner kept firing. But the first fighter was in close and scored a direct hit on the smuggler's ship. It disintegrated. They had no means of escaping the wrecked spaceship. All hands and passengers died immediately when the smuggler's cargo craft exploded.

* * *

And Nina was alone in the mountains.

CHAPTER 19
SPACEBORNE MARINES

Lieutenant Ben Scott and his platoon were somewhat cramped in their spaces on the spacecraft carrier. The entire regiment was aboard and lots of landing craft. Planetary invasion exercises were in progress. In fact it was more like a rehearsal for the real thing. Training wouldn't be this intense if something big wasn't in the mill but, of course, Ben had been told nothing.

The men were playing cards. The mess deck was full of men. The passageways were full of men. And there were marines on the hanger deck doing calisthenics. Each platoon had their turn at doing calisthenics on the hanger deck. Had to stay in shape.

Then after two weeks of unbearable confinement, Ben received orders to muster his men and get them ready to board landing craft. The planet Jen was an uninhabited planet and they were going to "invade" her.

So he had his men prepare for an equipment inspection. He wanted to make sure their weapons and gear were in order. Then after the inspection, the platoon filed down the passageway, down three ladders, and over to a landing craft. One platoon would fit inside one landing craft. A little crowded, but they would fit.

Then the pilots boarded and started their drives. They lifted the craft up 3 feet off the deck. The landing craft was maneuvered into the launch position. The hanger doors were opened and they launched into space. Down, down, down, to the planet surface. When they got below 10,000 feet, the yellow light came on. That meant get ready to bail out. Then when all men were ready, the ramp in the back opened and the green light came on. That meant it was time to jump. As platoon commander, Ben was the first one to jump. So Lieutenant Ben Scott ran down the ramp. He waited until he was well clear of the landing craft before he fired off his backpack rockets.

Sergeant Rohr, the platoon sergeant, would be the last one out.

He'd make sure all the men jumped and made it out okay. It was Sergeant Rohr's job to push the "done" button on the bulkhead just before he jumped to let the pilots know the marines were all out and that it was safe to close the ramp doors.

When Ben got down to about 5,000 feet he could see they had jumped over a desert. There were other men already on the ground. His landing craft wasn't the first one to launch. The entire regiment was jumping today.

There was an area of rocky and hilly terrain about 20 miles or so to their northwest. It was the "enemy fortifications" that they'd attack. And they would be defended by "enemy soldiers." They could see the rocks clearly from above. Ben landed. And it was soft sand. He looked up. The sky was full of marines. About three landing craft had already discharged paratroops shortly after his men jumped. The next marine landed near him.

"All right?" Ben called.

"Yes, sir," the marine answered.

After it looked like everyone in the platoon had reached the ground he went looking for Sergeant Rohr. He saw him land. He was the last one, of course. He walked over to him. And walking was difficult across the sand dunes.

"Hello, Sarge. Take a muster and check for casualties."

"Yes, sir," Sergeant Rohr told him. It was just a formality. The Sergeant knew the first thing he did after a jump was make sure all the men were okay.

In a few minutes, Sergeant Rohr came over and reported, "Two simulated casualties, sir. Two men with sprained ankles."

"Okay. Have the corpsmen get them to the field hospital. Get the men formed up and ready to march."

"Yes, sir," reported Sergeant Rohr. He didn't salute. You didn't salute officers while on maneuvers. An enemy sniper could discern from that which were officers.

The corpsmen carried two men on stretchers to a place where a field hospital was being set up. It was made up of tents and what not. After the medical officers and corpsmen drilled their procedures, the "wounded" men would be released and formed up as "walking wounded" and start their march toward the town. They'd join their outfit later and become "replacement" troops.

It was a twenty mile march. It was about 10 o'clock by the sun when they started. And they had to make it by nightfall. And Ben didn't see how they could, hiking through deep sand this way. The sand was ankle deep. Every man was already sweating and any breeze at all stirred up the sand. Everyone was covered with dust.

But on they slogged in ankle deep sand. Each carried a canteen. And they knew that their water had to last until the end of their march. They were halted for a 10 minute rest every two hours. Research had indicated that men could march longer and farther in a day if they had a break every two hours.

Almost everyone's canteen was empty by mid afternoon. And it was hot. Throats were dry. Plug, plug. Soft sand. Sultry heat. Ben was covered with sweat, in fact his clothes were soaked. Why did I choose the marines? Ben thought. If I had joined the Fleet like Vic and Dan I'd be sitting on a nice cool ship now with all the water I wanted to drink. But marines were marines. And he had to set an example for the men. So he had to try to pretend he was neither tired nor thirsty.

It was sundown before they finally halted for the night and made camp. They were still about 5 miles or so from the rocks. A ground car arrived and visited each platoon leaving off a barrel of water, rations and camping gear. Ben had his men line up at the barrel to fill their canteens. He was the last one to quench his thirst. Then they made camp which just consisted of eating cold rations. They had no fuel for a fire. I mean like this was *barren* desert. Nothing growing at all. After they'd eaten, the marines to go on watch were posted, and the rest of them rolled up inside their blankets without delay and conked out.

At least the sand is soft to sleep on, Ben found himself thinking as he drifted off to sleep.

* * *

At dawn they were up. With a quick breakfast of cold field rations and water they were rolling up their blankets and breaking camp, getting ready to launch their attack on the enemy fortifications. They hiked the last five miles with simulated shells bursting around them. They "ran" their zigzag patterns per regulation, except "staggered" rather than "ran" would have been a more a more accurate term. When they stopped to hit the dirt, which they had to do when the simulated shells hit, they had sand dunes to hide behind at least.

When they reached the rocks they were out of the sand. So it looked like they had firm ground to fight on. Then they swarmed into the rocks. The referees were posted to score kills. Ben moved up just over a rock to see an "enemy" in desert camouflage uniform except with a red beret to label him an enemy. Ben's regiment had on blue berets. He tagged him with a quick shot from his blast rife, which he had set on light fire. You'd barely feel it, but you'd know you were "hit." She fell just like she was supposed to. *She.*

The enemy soldier was a woman. Pretty soon they found that the entire defending force were women marines. The simulated fighting raged. Ben remembered they had been briefed not to engage in hand to hand fighting. So this was why. Hmmm.

Ben continued to wind his way through the rocks. He'd lost sight of his men because most of the rocks were taller than he. He heard talking. So he carefully slipped around a cluster of rocks over behind where the voices came from. He came up to an opening and saw three women with their back to him. One was talking on the radio.

"You are my prisoners," he said.

They all three jumped and turned around, grabbing for their blast pistols. Then they relaxed. He had them dead to rights. So he instructed them to remove their blast pistol belts and hand them to him. He had obviously captured a platoon commander. The woman in the middle was taller than the other two, also younger. She had a lieutenant's bars on her beret. The other two had sergeant's stripes on their sleeves. The lieutenant was a very nice looking woman.

After a few hours the fortress was secure. They had several hundred "prisoners" that were herded out onto the hot sand outside the rocks. And corpsmen were bringing out the simulated wounded so they'd get their practice in tending to them. They made their exercises as realistic as possible.

Then the exercise was secured. Ben knew they had women Fleet Marines and he knew that they had them formed up in different regiments than the men.

For now, Ben's platoon was covered with sweat and caked dirt. Ben got permission for his men to go to a nearby lake and get a bath. The rocky spot where they had their mock battle was about 3 or 4 miles from a mountain range. There was a creek that drained into a small lake. The water was shallow enough you could wade through most of it.

The entire regiment had the same idea. So when they went down to the water, stripped and waded in, it was full of marines. And Ben noted that about half the bathers were women marines. Most of them had changed to bikinis since they knew they'd be sharing their bathing facilities with men.

One female sergeant walked down to the bank, stripped off naked and just slowly waded into the water. She acted like she was oblivious of all the men. They didn't really stare, though. She wasn't all that well built. She was kind of stocky. She had big biceps and her body was muscular all over. She looked like she was in good physical condition, but not especially good looking. In fact, you could say she wasn't good looking at all.

When Ben finished washing off the dirt, he climbed back to the bank and put on his clothes. He had brought along some khaki shorts and a red T shirt. It was the marine athletic uniform that they wore when doing physical training. It also included sneakers. He headed back to camp. He was hungry by then.

CHAPTER 20
LADY LIEUTENANT

When he got back to camp, there was no one there. The officers camped separately from the men, of course. The pup tents had been set up and their blankets were laid out inside them, but the other officers were all gone.

The female regiment, of course, had their own camp, and Ben figured he had a pretty good idea where the men were at, including the other officers. So he wondered over to the women's camp. He went looking for the officer's tents. When he found them he saw a woman standing alone, near the fire, combing her hair. Her hair was wet. She was wearing khaki shorts and a red T-shirt, similar to his own uniform. She apparently had just gotten back from the bathing pond, too.

There was a rank insignia on the chest of the red/khaki uniform. A vertical bar meant lieutenant. She had a lieutenant's rank insignia. So she was the same rank as Ben. Ben walked up. "Hello, Lieutenant, Ma'am," Ben said.

She jumped, startled, because she didn't see him approach. When she saw him she noticed how good looking he was, and he didn't have an offensive manner, so she just said, "Hello yourself, Lieutenant, Sir."

"I was wondering where everyone was," he said. Then he recognized her. She was the platoon commander he had captured earlier that day.

"You!" she exclaimed as she recognized him, too.

"So we meet again," he said.

"It appears so. And this time hopefully in better circumstances," she replied.

"I wondered where everyone was at," he then said. "There's no one over in our camp."

"They're having a party tonight," she explained. "There's food over at the cook tent."

She was an exceptionally beautiful woman. Her khaki shorts were very short and they fit really snug. Her T shirt fit really snug, too, which made it clear she was a rather voluptuous lady. Her hair was the same color as her shorts. She had on white sox and white sneakers, as did Ben. "Where is the cook tent?" he asked. She gave him directions to the cook tent. So Ben left her standing there combing her hair.

In five minutes he was back with two paper plates of food and two paper cups of drink. He handed her one and went and sat down on a rock nearby. There were two big rocks with a flat surface. Nature made chairs. She accepted her plate and sat on the other rock and started eating. He hadn't asked her to eat with him. He just assumed she was hungry, too.

Ben started to realize how really starved he was when he started eating. She was starved, too, though her regiment didn't have nearly as rigorous an afternoon as the male regiment. The women were mainly just sitting and hiding behind rocks waiting for the "attackers" to show. But Ben noticed she had a frown on her face.

"You don't look happy," Ben told her.

"Well, you could have at least let us win," was her retort.

"Oh. That's what bothering you. You know Fleet Marines never let the other side win, even if they're women."

"I know," she said. She obviously wasn't nearly as mad as she was pretending to be.

"Lieutenant, Ma'am, I'll have to confess, those are the prettiest legs I've ever seen," he said blatantly.

"Lieutenant, Sir, I'll have to say the same for yours," she replied just as blatantly. Ben took a double take on that. He'd never had a woman tell him *his* legs were pretty.

"So your regiment just trains assault regiments, huh?" he wanted to get some kind of conversation going. She seemed kind of timid, though she wasn't acting like she resented his presence especially.

"Yes, that's our mission," she answered.

"And your regiment just camps out here all the time?"

"The camp for the enlisted women is actually on the other side of the rocks over toward the west," she explained. "There's a place where there aren't so many rocks where they pitch their pup tents. We're in the sand dunes here, because it's softer sleeping at night. There's a cluster of caves over in the mountains where we go when the wind gets up. The sand storms are horrible here. We're crowded when the entire regiment goes there for shelter against the wind, but we can survive a sand storm there." Ben knew how hot it got when the wind *didn't* get up. They had had no wind at all during their march over the sand dunes. Maybe his men were lucky, after all.

Then they heard music coming from over in the rocks. "Do they have a dance going on or something?" Ben asked.

"No," she replied. "The sand is too soft for a dance and there isn't room among the rocks, either. But they have a band to play for them. And some of the girls have musical instruments. I have a uke, but I don't know how to play it, yet. Do you know how to play?"

"Actually I do play a uke a little bit," he answered. She laid down her plate and cup and went to a pup tent. She came back and handed him a uke. A small stringed instrument with nylon strings. Ben tuned it.

He struck up a tune and started singing. "Hey, you sing!" she was surprised. She'd finished eating by then. After a couple of songs she joined in with him on the chorus.

Ben had finished eating by then, too, and they had finished their drinks. Ben took his paper cup and hers and went back over to the cook tent and filled them. Then he came back and handed her drink to her.

"What's your name?" he asked.

"Lisa Mann," she replied. "Yours?"

"Ben Scott," he answered. Then he started up another tune. He found out she knew a lot of the same songs that he knew. She was sitting on the rock with her side to him and her legs crossed. She really presented a sexy image sitting there. She had done her hair up on top of her head. Ben just figured he'd keep his cool. He didn't want to make a bad impression. He'd never seen a woman this beautiful before.

"You know a lot of the same songs as I know," he observed. "Where are you from?"

"Ultaria," she explained, "But my father was from Armenia. He

82

escaped from the Old Empire on a smuggler's ship. He works in a factory in Seaside. He wanted me to get an education. So he worked and slaved so I could go to school. I was bored with the life there at Seaside and joined the Fleet Marines looking for adventure. Father was disappointed that I didn't want to go to college. He still works at the same factory."

"Have you found the adventure you were looking for?" he was now curious.

"I guess I have," she said. "At least it's different. I seldom feel bored."

"I'm keeping you from the party," he said. "Do you wish I'd leave so you could join the others?"

"Are you wanting to go to the party?" she was completely noncommittal.

"No, of course not," he quickly explained. "I'd rather be here with you."

"They get rather boisterous at the parties. I'd like to hear you sing some more." Ben liked her answer.

Ben took their cups over to the cook tent and filled them again, then came back and picked up the uke again. The drinks were obviously alcoholic because he was feeling them by now. But he liked to play and sing and he noted that Lisa had a very beautiful voice. She did a terrific job singing harmony for him.

They sang and played for hours. When it was well after midnight, Ben got up, reached over and took Lisa's hand, paused a moment, then helped her up.

"Where are you taking me?" she asked.

"Which tent is yours?" he answered with a question. She pointed to it. He started to lead her to it, and she hung back. He paused a moment and then started leading her toward her tent again. She didn't resist this time. He led her to her tent and took her inside. Both of them were pretty high by this time. He arranged the blankets and put her inside them. Then, underneath the covers, he removed her shoes and sox. Then her shorts and T shirt. Then he pulled off her bra and panties before he removed his own clothes. Heaven, was all he could think of.

* * *

When Ben woke, Lisa was still sleeping. He got up and put his shorts and T-shirt back on. Then he put on his socks and shoes. He didn't want to wake her. But he wanted to get her message code before leaving. Then he remembered hearing her say her platoon was the 3rd Platoon of F Company. He could reach her through her platoon. Dawn was barely showing in the sky. He went back to the men's camp.

He arrived at the officer's camp for his regiment and changed to his camouflage uniform and boots. He received orders from the company commander to get the men ready to move out. And he looked his men over. They were obviously hung over and several of them had bruises and black eyes. So a couple of them obviously had been in a fight the night before. This was what always happened when men and women got a chance to mix. Discipline deteriorated. But men just naturally wanted to seek out the women. And vice versa. And invariably, two men would want the same woman. So black eyes and bruises was the result. Ben actually didn't mind their fighting tendency. He wanted fighting men. But he didn't want them fighting each other. Their purpose was to fight the enemy.

Ben got his platoon loaded into one of the landing craft and they took off, headed back to the mother ship.

CHAPTER 21
DEPLOYMENT

The following morning was a Monday, of course. Vic found out that he had received new orders. He had orders to deploy on board a spacecraft carrier with a fighter squadron. That meant he would have to leave Red. He also felt a sense of dread because he didn't know what was to come. He didn't like it, but what could he do? Orders are Orders. He had until the end of the month before he'd have to leave.

When he got home that night and told Red, her jaw dropped. She assumed a forlorn look on her face and said, "What?"

He had kind of a long face, too. He enjoyed Red's company *so* much! She wanted to know how long he had before he had to leave and he told her. Then her next question was "Why?"

"I'm sure the reason for a spacecraft carrier's deployment is classified. They haven't even told me. But there's apparently something going on somewhere in the galaxy in which experienced fighter pilots will be needed."

Red didn't like the sound of that at all. And Vic wished he'd worded it differently. But he just took her by the hand, led her to the couch, sat down and pulled her into his lap. He just held her and explained that this what the life of a spacecraft fighter pilot was like. He would have to deploy at times in the years to come, and then he would rotate to planet side duty again, hopefully for several years at a time.

Somehow, now that they knew he was leaving, they wanted to make the best of the time they did have left. Vic took Red dancing several times during the week. And he took her out to dinner more than once a week, too. And they took another trip out to their remote island on the Big Lake again, as soon as it was Sunday and Vic got a day off. Vic decided to start teaching Red how to fly the flying saucer since he'd be leaving it with her while he was gone.

After three and a half weeks, it was time for him to pack his gear and report to the base spaceport. Red had learned how to fly his flying saucer by then. At least well enough to get by. So they flew to the space port and landed in the public parking area. She walked with him to the gate. They had some time before boarding time, so they just stood and talked. Then when they received the call to board the troop shuttle he gave her one big hug and kiss and put his space bag on his shoulder and walked through the gate toward the troop shuttle. Red stood with tears streaming down her face watching him walk up the ramp. She watched him till he was nearly out of site. Then he stopped, turned and waved and she waved back, trying to hide her tears.

The troop shuttle took off and after about two hours, it arrived at the mother ship. Vic was assigned a state room. He checked with his squadron communication officer and found out he could send message disks to friends and relatives. They'd be censored but that was alright. So he got a message disk off to Red his first night in space. Then he continued to send her a message daily. She responded to each one very promptly. They used message disks by putting a video/audio message on a disk. Then removing the disk from the machine you would put it in a sleeve and place it in an envelope and drop it into the mail sack. The mail would be either placed on a cargo vessel, or if there was a lot of mail, a mail ship would be dispatched to and from the home planet.

In the meantime, training exercises were scheduled to get the pilots transitioned to shipboard operations. Spacecraft launching and recovery are the first skills to be addressed. Each squadron was scheduled for a block of time, usually about two hours each day, and during that two hours they just practiced launching out into space and then returning and making an approach to a landing in the landing bay. The ship had four landing bays on each side.

After about a dozen or so launches and recoveries for each pilot he was considered spacecraft carrier qualified. Then they would just launch and fly patrol from about 500 miles to several thousand miles away from the ship. Six squadrons had fighter craft that were space borne at all times. The space around the ship was divided into six sectors. Above the ship, below, left and right, forward of the ship and behind the ship.

Six of the squadrons on board were fighter squadrons and six of them were strike squadrons. The strike spacecraft were a little larger than the fighter craft and carried a crew of two: pilot and navigator/bombardier. The strike craft could fire laser torpedoes or drop laser bombs, as well as send out a laser blast from a nose gun. They could also use high explosive armament if it was deemed more practical. At least one of the strike squadrons would launch on a training strike mission every day and the fighter escort spacecraft they would normally use on such a mission launched with them and did their simulated dog fighting as part of the training exercise. But there were also the patrols of fighter craft necessary around the clock whether there was a strike exercise in progress or not. So the strike exercise escort mission was in addition to the routine patrols.

Vic had a full flight schedule. When he wasn't flying patrol for the mother ship he was engaged in a training exercise escorting strike spacecraft. He barely had time to eat and get enough sleep.

CHAPTER 22
JULES MEETS NINA

Jules worked his way down the trail to the place where the refugees had camped. Not that he intended to camp there. But he had cached some of his supplies in a small cave on the far side of the camp and it was more convenient to take the same trail. He couldn't retrieve them until the refugees had left since he didn't want its location known. There was no evidence of any Imperial troops in the area.

The abandoned refugee camp had been located in a low area at the base of a mountain. It was like a large bowl sunk below the surrounding terrain. Almost no grass grew there and no trees. The surrounding area was covered with tall, green deciduous trees. He was walking by and headed up the mountain trail to a place where the small cave with his cache was located.

As he walked by the camp he looked over and saw a girl in ragged, baggy pants and a dirty sweatshirt with a water bag on each shoulder and a very forlorn look on her face. She started to scream when she saw Jules but then she recognized him. She threw her water bags down and ran to him.

"And why are you still here?" he said when she put her arms around his neck with relief all over her face. He had a deep timber to his voice.

"I went to get water to cook with," she explained.

"Well, you missed your ship," he told her.

She looked downcast again. "I didn't know the ship had arrived. We weren't told exactly when the ship would be here. And it was time to start cooking."

"You can catch the next ship," he then returned. "Your passage was paid for. The captain of the next ship can get it from the captain of this ship. The captains of some of the smuggling ships work together. Not all of them do." Of course Jules had no idea that the spacecraft of refugees was no more.

"But what will I do until then?" the forlorn look was back on her face.

"You can stay with me until another group of refugees gathers."

He then told her to pick up the water bottles she had dropped. He stooped and retrieved a couple of blankets she had left on the ground. He rolled them up and tossed them over his shoulder. Then he told her to follow him. She noticed that he had a crossbow in a sling over his shoulder as they started up the trail.

There was nothing else he could do. He couldn't leave her there. But why do I have to get saddled with something like this? he thought. It was a complication he didn't need.

When they walked up the trail near to the cave where his cache was located, he just walked on by. He'd have to replenish the supplies in his backpack later. The less she knew about his secret caches, the better. So he just continued to lead her up the trail. He knew that they needed to get far away from this place. It might have been compromised by now.

When it was nearly sundown Jules found a place to make camp.

CHAPTER 23
THE POWER

Vic was sitting in the ready room, getting briefed for his flight. The squadron intelligence officer was doing the briefing.

"The people that live on this planet are still in the bronze age. They do have primitive tools. We are setting up our base on a continent that has not been discovered by the populace of the planet. They have wooden ships but are afraid to get out of sight of land so it is predicted that they won't discover this continent for at least another thousand years.

"Your job? You will be flying escort missions for transport craft that will land and off load material and supplies for our new base which is being built there. It has not been conquered yet by the Old Empire so it is classified as a neutral planet. Since we will not be making war against the local populace it doesn't violate our policy of respecting the governments of neutral planets. Our base is currently about three fourths complete."

It was obvious to Vic why they were using the transport craft instead of the larger cargo vessels. They were faster and more maneuverable though they couldn't carry as much. But they were heavily armed themselves and could evade enemy fire more effectively than larger vessels could.

"The transports will load up at the planet Misten. Misten is a planet with a well developed mining industry and the smelting plants and factories needed to manufacture the supplies and equipment needed. You will escort the transports, who will fly in convoys, from the planet Misten to the planet where the base is being built."

Vic sat through the briefing and then it came time to man spacecraft. And Vic noticed he had that jittery feeling in his belly again. He didn't know what they'd come up against out there. He walked down the passageway to the hanger bay. He found his fighter craft and climbed in. He put on his space suit and strapped in. Then he got the signal from the deck director to start engines.

In a few minutes he was out the hanger bay door and joining up with his flight of four fighter craft. They flew to the area where the transport spacecraft were traveling in a convoy of four transport craft. They had just taken off with their load of supplies from the planet Misten and were en route to their destination. Vic's flight took up station just behind the transports as briefed. He had completely forgotten about the jittery feeling by now.

The first patrol was uneventful. But on the second day out, Vic saw unfriendly pips on his EWD (early warning detection) scope. He immediately made a report on his radio to the flight leader and changed course to head for them.

When he was within range he saw the laser bursts from the enemy ships and immediately started taking evasive action. He managed to get an enemy plane in his sights and fired. It disappeared off his scope. That's one! He had to evade some more shots fired at him and then he managed to shoot down another. Then he was amongst the enemy ships and he had the added problem of making sure he didn't shoot at his own forces.

He knew he had to just do the best he could and identify each target on his screen as enemy before firing at them. At the same time he had to make sure he got in firing position for any that he did identify as enemy craft. He scored a kill. Then he maneuvered quickly and got in position to shoot down another enemy spacecraft. Then laser bursts were all around him and he had to spend all his time evading enemy fire for several minutes.

He got in position to shoot another enemy fighter craft down, but instead of shooting, he jinked quickly. Just barely in time to avoid a direct hit. He turned and fired at the spacecraft that shot at him and the pip disappeared from his screen. Then he jinked again just barely in time to avoid being hit.

He found out he was anticipating the enemy laser fire a second or two in advance! Nothing on his detection gear could him saved him from the past two near misses. This can only happen if you have the "power!"

The battle raged for hours and Vic continued to evade hit after hit. He had to pass up many chances to shoot down enemy fighter

Randell K. Whaley

craft to avoid being hit, but he still scored quite a few kills. Too many to count.

When the enemy spacecraft finally retreated and left the area he was exhausted. He was very eager to see the relief patrol arrive so he could return to the mother ship.

* * *

Vic was on station with his fighter craft again. So far there had been no contacts with unknown forces. Then a voice came up on the radio. "All spacecraft fighters take up station along the route on the right of the transport convoy." It was the flight leader's voice. Vic knew that if intelligence sources indicated that an attack was most likely in a given sector that they were to maneuver over in that direction as soon as possible. Vic knew there was the risk of the enemy trying to lure them over to the other side by a feint. So they had to be ready to move back to their original position very quickly if necessary.

They started jinking back and forth while repositioning their fighter craft to make it harder for someone to ambush them if that was their purpose. Then Vic saw a flood of enemy pips on his screen. He immediately turned and locked onto an enemy fighter and fired his laser. The enemy pip disappeared. A kill. And it looked like he had drawn first blood in the engagement though the other fighters were getting into position to shoot as quickly as they could. With violent maneuvering and using all his instincts plus the "power", Vic knocked out at least half a dozen enemy fighters and had at least that many near misses.

But it's different if you are shot at simultaneously by three enemy fighters. He was warned by the "power" and out maneuvered two of them. But the second maneuver put him right in line with the third laser burst and it got his spacecraft. Knocked out both his main drives and set his ship on fire. He was already in his pressure suit as was the standard procedure while in battle but he had to push a button to get his escape capsule to come down and fasten. He hit his ejection button and his escape capsule fired. It was like being shot out of the bore of a cannon but he managed to get clear of his spacecraft before it exploded. His capsule had rockets to give him some control of his direction and speed. And he knew where the nearest habitable planet was. It would be better if he could get rescued by Search and Rescue forces right where he was, but there was a fat chance of that happening while the battle was raging. He saw the planet taking shape. As he got closer he maneuvered so the bottom of his capsule was toward the planet. This put his head in the opposite direction. He could look down and could see the planet surface okay. The capsule was made of a strong, thick, transparent type of material. Not glass, but of a synthetic material that was shatterproof.

When he got down well within the atmosphere he saw blue water and the green of several continents. He adjusted the path of his descent to make sure he would come down over land.

He knew that this was a primitive planet. In fact the human population was in the "cave man" phase in its development. That had been covered in their survival briefing at the beginning of the mission. All the likely planets for forced landings or ejections in their area of operation were all listed and they had to memorize them and their stage of civilization development as part of their survival training.

He kept floating down, firing his rockets as necessary. They served as retro rockets from the attitude of the capsule, since his tail was toward the planet. He saw that he was descending down into a mountainous area. He finally landed. He knew the planet had a breathable atmosphere, or course. Cave men couldn't live here if it didn't. He removed his pressure suit before making his exit of the escape capsule. His pressure suit was bright silver and would show up good which wouldn't be bad if search and rescue craft were searching for him. But it sure was hot with it on.

Chapter 24
Cave Man

He left his pressure suit inside the escape capsule when he climbed out and found his survival pack that was under the seat. He opened it. There was a survival belt with a blast pistol, canteen full of water, survival knife and radio. He put that on first. Then there was a back pack. It had things like emergency rations and a blanket which folded up really small but would keep him from freezing at night. He left the radio beeper off for now. He turned it to receive only. It had a vibrater feature that would make it start to vibrate as soon as transmissions from the SAR (search and rescue) spacecraft were within range. The enemy spacecraft could intercept it so the SAR forces wouldn't begin their search until the battle was over and the enemy cleared from the area. After the battle was over the SAR spacecraft would start searching for survivors of any lost spacecraft. So he'd have to wait a few hours. When he felt his belt radio start vibrating, he would turn his radio beeper on and it would send out a signal that the SAR spacecraft could zero in on and find his location.

For now he set out to find a place to camp. He had a canteen of water but he knew that wouldn't last long. He needed to find a stream or creek. And he didn't know if he'd meet a native or not or if they'd be hostile. Intelligence reports indicated that man on this planet were cave men who didn't even have metal knives to cut with. They were strictly hunters who lived on meat but had to use a sharp rock to skin and cut up their game.

Vic wasn't used to walking long distances. Sure, they had some pretty vigorous physical training back when he first started space flight training back in the Old Empire. But that was a year or more ago. He wasn't in such terrific physical condition now. After a couple of hours he started feeling tired. And the trail he was following was a mountain trail, up and down continuously.

Then he came upon a creature and stopped suddenly. He drew his blast pistol. It looked like a monster at first. It was 7 1/2 feet tall and had huge arms and shoulders. It had a beard that went half way down to its waist and black matted hair about as long going down his back. It was obviously male. He was wearing an animal skin that hung from one shoulder. He had a huge club drawn back ready to strike. But something told him to hold his fire.

Something told him this creature wasn't really hostile. He was just prepared to defend himself as he himself was willing to do. So he lowered his blast pistol. The cave man relaxed his club and let it rest on his shoulder. They had standing orders not to do any harm to any of the planet's habitants except in self defense.

He knew he wouldn't know the cave man's language but in survival training in the Old Empire he had been taught the universal sign language that all primitive people used on planets such as this. And the presence of the "power" became apparent, too. He could sense that the man was afraid of him but also curious. He was just naturally suspicious of strangers. He fastened his blast pistol back to his belt and used sign language to explain to him that he wanted to be a friend. The cave man responded with the same sign language that that was what he wanted, too.

He told the cave man that he was looking for a place to camp near water. The cave man motioned for him to follow. He then turned and walked to a dead animal lying on the ground. It was a four legged creature. It looked similar to a sheep but without the wool. It looked like it weighed probably a hundred pounds or more. He picked it up with one hand like as if it weighed no more than a rabbit, placed it on his shoulder and started walking. Vic followed him.

Vic had difficulty keeping up with him. His companion was apparently accustomed to traveling along mountain trails. They walked for a couple of hours. Vic was soaked in sweat by then and his legs felt like rubber. He looked at the sun. It was about noon.

Then finally they came to a camp. Smoke was rising from a camp fire. The fire was near the entrance to what appeared to be a cave. He saw a woman dressed in an animal skin garment. It was similar to what the man wore except it appeared to be made out of leopard skin. Her hair was matted and tangled. She wasn't especially pretty but she wasn't fat. Her garment barely covered her hips and buttocks. Her legs were hairy but fairly well shaped.

"Aba," the cave man said, pointing to her.

"Vic", Vic said, pointing to himself.

"Og," the cave man said, pointing to himself.

Then the cave man laid down his kill. He untied what looked like two raw hide strings that had held the body cavity together. He apparently had already field dressed it but wanted to hold the body cavity closed while carrying it home. He put his hand inside and pulled out what looked like liver. He handed it to the woman. She squealed with delight and grabbed it. She put it to her mouth and took a bite out of and started chewing with obvious relish. She had a look of ecstasy on her face.

So raw liver was her favorite food, Vic concluded. The liver was still bloody. She had blood on her mouth and hands and seemed oblivious of it. The way she went after it, Vic figured she probably hadn't eaten in days.

Then Og reached in and pulled out another piece of organ meat and offered it to Vic. Using sign language, Vic explained that he preferred just red meat only, and then only when it was cooked. So Og skinned back a haunch and with a piece of sharp rock, cut it around the joint, then with pure brute strength wrenched it loose from the carcass. Then he placed it on top of a tripod of sticks placed over the fire so it could cook. Then he sat down and motioned Vic to do the same. He took a bite out of the piece of organ meat he had offered Vic. Sweetbread, maybe, Vic thought.

Then with one hand, the cave man asked Vic where he came from. He didn't dare answer "the sky" which would be the truth. He was afraid he'd scare the man more than he had on their first meeting. He just answered, "Far away."

Then Og asked him what he hunted. He apparently wanted to talk. Lonesome for company? Og's wife was still kneeling by the fire consuming her raw liver with obvious delight. He knew that liver was very nourishing. It probably had all the food value that they needed. And he had noticed that the liver had a piece cut off of it when he first pulled it out and handed it to her. Or a piece bit off of it. So Og must have assuaged his own hunger shortly after making his kill. And then he apparently saved most of the liver for his wife.

Og was curious about his clothing. Vic, of course, had his flight suit on under his pressure suit and that was what he was wearing now. Vic explained that he had traded for it. It wasn't a lie exactly. His uniforms were provided by the Fleet. And he worked for the Fleet. So the food, clothing and pay were things traded for his service to the Fleet.

In a few minutes another person started walking up, carrying two animal skin bags, one on each shoulder. It appeared to be female, in fact she was a carbon copy of Aba only appeared to be much younger. She was probably a teenager. So she must be Og's daughter, he thought. She walked to a dwarfy tree a little distance from the fire. Vic then noticed the mouth of a cave nearby. She placed one of the animal skin bottles on a limb of the tree and then brought the other to her father. He pulled a piece of wooden plug out of the end of it that apparently served as a cork and took a drink out of it. Then he offered it to Vic. Vic politely declined and showed him his canteen.

"Eba," Og said, pointing to his daughter. "Bick," he said, pointing to Vic. It appeared that Og had manners and was conscientious about observing some form of protocol. And Eba bowed slightly when introduced. It was almost like a curtsey. He was more than amused. They were very interesting, these cave men and women. They had manners and customs just like civilized people.

Og took another piece of organ meat out of the body cavity of the animal and handed it to his daughter. She squealed with excitement very much the same as her mother had and took a bite out of it. She rolled the piece of bloody meat on her tongue with ecstasy. Then she went and sat down by her mother and continued eating. So this is how a cave man provided for his family. He brought them meat which they would eat raw. But he did have a camp fire and he was roasting a haunch of meat. So he apparently knew how to build a fire and cook meat, too.

After the girls had finished eating, they came and joined the men. They sat with their knees under them. That must be a comfortable position for a woman, Vic thought. But he noticed that Og sat with his knees apart and his feet together in a fashion similar to how Vic was sitting.

But before Aba sat down she took hold of the sides of the skirt of her mini dress and pulled them out to the side as if she wanted to show it to him. Similar to how a civilized woman would do! He wondered if it was a new dress.

Then Og started describing a hunt he had gone on. Vic was really glad he had been taught universal sign language. Og was describing a fight with a leopard. That apparently was where Aba's leopard skin dress came from. By the time Og had finished his story, Vic figured out what was being communicated to him. To prove himself a man in this cave man society you had to kill a leopard. And a leopard skin dress was a status symbol for a woman. It meant she was married to a man that was very brave and a skilled hunter. The man didn't always win a fight with a leopard. Sometimes the leopard won. Of course, that meant the woman would become a young widow. When Og described the leopard he indicated its height to be about 6 feet tall at the shoulders. Vic could believe him. It had been covered in his survival lectures that they had large leopards on this planet.

The meat that was cooking was done enough to eat. Og started to cut off a piece of it with his piece of sharp rock. Then Vic took out his belt knife and cut off a piece of it and handed it to Og. He cut off another piece and handed it to Aba. He didn't really know the chain of command in a cave man family. He was just guessing. But after he cut off a piece of meat for Eba and handed it to her, he handed the knife to Aba. He explained with sign language that it was a present.

She exclaimed with delight and held it up for everyone to see. Vic knew that the women were the ones that had to skin and butcher the meat in a cave man family. That was covered in his training. The man was a hunter and brought home the meat. He cautioned Aba that the knife was very sharp and to not cut herself. He didn't really think it was that sharp himself. The survival knives issued didn't take an edge that well. Some of the pilots bought hunting knives from sporting goods stores so they'd have a knife that you could sharpen really well. But it would be much sharper than the sharp pieces of rock she was used to.

Since he was giving out presents, he figured he'd better think of something for the daughter and father, too. He took a signal mirror out of his pack and gave it to Og. He showed him how it worked. He showed him how you could make a light shine on a rock or tree if you wanted. And you could look in it if you wanted and see the same thing you'd see if you looked into a stream. Og was delighted but didn't show his excitement nearly as vigorously as the women.

Vic found a spare belt buckle in his gear and a piece of string. It was made of bronze. He threaded the string through it and went and tied it around Eba's neck. Then he held it up to her so she could see how shiny it was. She was ecstatic! She got up and danced around and around! So cave women go nuts over jewelry, too, just like modern women do.

Vic still had felt no vibrations coming from his radio. So he just continued to take a bite out of the meat that Og had given him every few minutes and chew on it. Meat was meat, though he liked it better with salt.

After Vic finished his piece of meat, Og started to cut off another piece for him when his wife jumped as if to say, "No, let me do it." She took her new knife and cut off a nice steak and handed it to Vic with a smile. He accepted it and smiled back. He could come to love these people. They were so friendly and accommodating. And hospitable.

Then he thought about how her knife would become dull with use. He took a whet stone out of his survival gear. He explained to Aba how the knife would become dull with time and showed her how to sharpen it. Then he handed her the whetstone and told her it was part of her present.

After he had finished his second piece of meat, he felt the signal coming from his radio. SAR aircraft were now searching for survivors. He reached down and turned his beeper on so he could send out a signal that the rescue spacecraft could pick up. Og, Aba and Eba were startled with the new noise. He pulled the radio from his belt and showed it to them. They looked at it curiously.

After another few minutes a voice came over the radio, "Vic."

"Vic here," Vic said into the radio.

Og very quickly repositioned his body into a kneeling position. Aba and Eba were already kneeling. They bowed down low and started a cooing noise in unison. He hadn't intended this. They apparently thought him a god or something. To be able to talk to a box and have it talk back.

"We're on our way," came the voice.

"Good," replied Vic. "Let me know when you're ready to land and I'll come and meet you."

"Roger," the voice replied.

The nearest place where a landing craft could land was at a ledge about 200 yards or so away. They'd have his coordinates from his beeper radio signal. When the SAR pilot on the radio called him again, he got up, said goodbye to the friendly cave man family and started walking away. At first they just watched him go in awe. Then they followed. When Vic reached the SAR aircraft and a ladder was lowered, he climbed into the SAR spacecraft. He looked back to see the cave man family on their knees bowing and cooing again.

When Vic got back to the mother ship he found out he had 30 days of quarantine before he could resume his duties. And he was reprimanded for eating the meat offered by the cave man. While it amounted to 30 days of solitary confinement, and was very boring, he could still send message disks to Red. Her answer to his first message made it clear that she was flooded with relief. He had been reported as "missing in action." She was afraid he had been killed or something. He answered her message and explained what had happened. He continued to send her a message daily. And she answered each one promptly. It was refreshing to look at her beautiful face on his video/audio player/recorder. She explained that she missed him and when was he going to finally come home?

CHAPTER 25
BACK ON DUTY

When Vic got back on board the spacecraft carrier, he was placed in his quarantine quarters immediately. Within a few hours a medical officer came down and gave him an examination. He wanted to make sure he had no injuries or illnesses initially, of course. Then Vic didn't see the MO any more for two weeks. Fourteen days to be exact. The medical officer explained that the minimum incubation period for any disease germ on that planet was fourteen days. He gave him another check up. Then he got a medical exam daily for a week.

In the meantime he was allowed to continue to send and receive message disks. He sent Red a disk describing to her his experience with having to eject from his spacecraft and float down to a planet. Then he described the cave man experience to her. He received a disk back from her the next day expressing her amazement about his experience with the cave man society. The picture of her talking to him looked so beautiful. She apparently always touched up her makeup and hair just before making him a disk. She had lots of questions, like what did the cave women wear? And what did they eat? Did the women do the cooking? Did they have a religion?

He sent her back a disk answering her questions. The religious question was complicated. They seemed to worship him, he explained. But it wasn't until he pulled out his radio and talked to the SAR forces that they seemed to think he was a god. He explained about the leopard skin dress the cave man's wife wore and its significance. And about the daughter going to the spring to get water for the family. And the woman's delight at receiving a hunting knife as a gift to make it easier skinning animals and cutting meat. And how the daughter was ecstatic about the make shift necklace he gave her. Red's next message indicated that she was absolutely enthralled with his experience. She wished he could take her to visit the cave man's family sometime.

At the end of the 30 day quarantine the medical officer gave him one more medical checkup. He gave him a clean bill of health and he returned to full duty. He had a new fighter craft assigned to him. At least it was new to him. It's previous pilot had brought it back damaged, himself severely wounded. He had been evacuated back to the hospital at the home planet and his spacecraft had been repaired.

So Vic was back to flying escort missions for the transport ships again. Since he had been shot down and rescued he was something of a celebrity. And everyone wanted to hear about his experience with the cave man's family. Some of the pilots couldn't resist the impulse to tease him. In fact, he had earned the nick name *Caveman* for a time. Then the part of the story about the cave man and his family thinking he was a god finally got around. So they started calling him *The Deity*. But for the pilots with religious tendencies that struck them as sacrilegious so that nickname didn't stick very long.

The enemy did attack the transport vessels again. Apparently they continued to learn the route that Vic's ship was taking over and over again, in spite of the fact that they changed it for each trip. More dogfights did occur. Vic continued to demonstrate his prowess as a fighter pilot over and over. In fact he scored three more kills in his next air battle.

Vic continued to send message disks to Red every few days. He explained that he missed her. And she sent messages back that she missed him.

Chapter 26
Overwhelm

Vic saw them on his EWD gear before they appeared on his view screen. Hundreds of enemy fighter craft. He immediately headed his ship toward them and notified the squadron commander on the radio. As soon as he was within range of the enemy spacecraft, he picked out a target and fired, then started jinking vigorously. Then he steadied out long enough to pick out another target and fired again. He saw it explode on his screen. He continued repeating this sequence of events. He lost count of the kills he scored but they kept coming.

Re-enforcements arrived from the ship as every squadron scrambled. It looked like it was going to be impossible to fight them all off. Then he saw some of the enemy ships start turning the other direction. It looked like they were going to drive them off! Then wham! His spacecraft was hit! And he felt the impact on his left arm and shoulder. But his ship kept flying. It was damaged but the hull hadn't been penetrated. It had knocked loose a black box from the bulkhead which struck his arm and shoulder a very solid blow. He called his flight leader and explained that he was hit and was heading for the spacecraft carrier.

He was almost overwhelmed with nausea at first. He was afraid he'd pass out. Then the nausea passed and he started sweating. And his noticed his whole left side was numb. No pain, just numb. And he felt groggy. He was flying with just one hand, now. It seemed to take forever to reach the ship. Then it occurred to him to check and see if there was any blood on his arm. He looked down at his arm which was hanging uselessly. It was swollen to about twice its normal size, but no, he didn't see any blood. He knew it would be covered with horrendous bruises.

He finally saw the open landing bay ahead of him. He had to reach over his left arm with his right arm to pull back the throttle to slow down his ship. When you pulled the throttle back to a certain point retro rockets automatically fired to make it possible for the ship to slow down. He eased it on in. It was a good thing he could land in his sleep because that was just about what he was doing, now. When he finally brought his spacecraft to rest on the flight deck, he passed out.

He woke up in sick bay feeling groggy. At first, he was aware only of the warmth of the room and the whiteness of the sheets. Then it dawned on him to look over to his left side. A white cast covered his left arm and shoulder. His arm was suspended from a piece of line to some kind of structure hanging over his bed.

After a few minutes a corpsman came in. He checked his vital signs. He looked down and asked "How do you feel?"

"Groggy," Vic answered.

"Gotcha. You just came out of surgery so you have a right to feel groggy."

The corpsman took the gurney that Vic was lying on and moved it out the door and down the passageway. He stopped at one of the patient compartments and wheeled him in. So he woke up in the recovery room. Later the medical officer came and paid him a visit. He explained to him he had a broken shoulder and had three fractures in his left upper arm. And that he was going to be evacuated to the home planet.

He couldn't say he felt good physically. His arm and shoulder had a steady ache in them. But he tried to keep this a secret from the doctor because he didn't want any more dope than he had to take. The next day he was moved to a hospital ship.

He learned that the hospital ship had left the combat sector. He was on his way home. He was elated with that thought. But he was mostly groggy and slept most of the time. And he found out he couldn't do without the dope. The pain got too bad when the drug wore off. So he found himself asking the corpsman for another shot when it got too bad. It would make him groggy all over again and he'd go to sleep again. But the medical officer had explained that he needed the sleep. That's when healing takes place the most efficiently is while you're sleeping.

They brought him food and he wasn't hungry. The corpsman told him he needed to eat. At first he was allowed to turn down food because the medical officer figured maybe his digestion system wasn't ready to take on food, yet. But after two days, the corpsman insisted that he at least have a bowl of hot soup. So he managed to do so. When the medical officer came by to check on him when making his rounds, he explained it was the pain reliever drugs that curbed his appetite. But he was giving him the drug with the least side effects. He should just force himself to eat until he could do without the pain killers.

Vic started going longer and longer without asking for a pain killer shot. He'd just bear the pain instead. But at night he couldn't sleep because of the pain so he'd let the corpsman give him a shot.

After a week Vic was able to do without the pain killer shots completely. He breathed a sigh of relief at that. He knew it was possible to become addicted.

CHAPTER 27
RED HEADED NURSE

The hospital ship landed on Ultaria at Seaside. His left arm and shoulder were still in a cast. There were two corpsmen waiting to take him to the base hospital. They put him on a gurney and wheeled him into the hospital and up to a room.

After an hour, Red walked into his room. "You didn't tell me you were coming home!" she sounded angry.

"I wasn't thinking very clearly when we left. I was on medication that kept me groggy."

"Oh," she said and calmed down. She walked over to his bed to reach down for a kiss. "It's so good to see you! And I've been so worried ever since I found out you were wounded. I was told you were reported missing in action, first. Then I learned that they found you. Then I got a message that you were wounded!" He had her listed as his next of kin to be notified in case anything happened to him.

"I'm getting along good. Doc says my arm will be good as new within a couple of months."

The next day she came by and brought with her a duffle bag to carry his stuff. "You're coming home with me," she told him.

"That's the best idea you've come up with all day," he replied. Since she had just walked in the door, it was her first idea of the day, so it was a dry jest. But Red had a lot of influence. Being the daughter of an admiral had its advantages.

When they got to Red's apartment, she put him straight to bed. "The doctor briefed me on what to do. You're to stay in bed for at least another two days. After that you can get up for short periods of time. And the doc wants you to come by to see him after those two days." He got the idea that she was really thrilled at having an excuse to be bossy, because she was never bossy. Maybe it was just because she didn't have an excuse before except in social situations and she wasn't really bossy then. She could assume a leadership role when needed without appearing to be bossy.

After a couple of days he was up and taking walks around the neighborhood. He started with just short walks, at first. He'd slowly make his way back to the apartment exhausted after fifteen minutes. He made his trip to see the medical officer at the base hospital after the two days were past and was told he was progressing fine.

He couldn't play his uke, but Red would play and sing to him in the evenings. And she cooked all his favorite dishes. And she kissed him every five minutes. In fact he felt like he was being smothered with affection. Maybe he should get wounded more often. He liked the results.

One evening after dinner, he and Red were sitting on the couch and he heard her sniffle. He looked over and saw she was crying. Now he couldn't think of a single thing for her to cry about. His arm and shoulder were healing nicely. It was his left arm and she was sitting on his right. He looked toward her and just looked at her for a minute. Then he said, "What is wrong?"

"Nothing," she said, but she kept on crying.

"Well, tell me what's making you cry."

"I want a baby," she said. She had stopped sniffling by now. "And I need a tissue." She got up and got a piece of tissue paper and wiped her eyes and blew her nose.

"We'll have to get married, first," he said. "You know I mustn't get you pregnant before our trial marriage is up."

"Yes, but there's no time limit on the trial marriage," she said.

"Are you already pregnant?" he asked.

"No, I've been taking birth control. I wouldn't be dishonest or sneaky with you. I'd get your agreement first before getting pregnant."

"I like the idea of you having us a baby. You could have us a daughter with red hair and green eyes just like yours."

"No! I want to have to a son! And daddy would have a fit if it wasn't a boy."

"Have you talked to the admiral about it?"

"Yes, of course I have. He wants a grandson. I told him I didn't want to rush my man. I really wanted to wait until you told me *you* wanted a baby. And I didn't mean to start crying tonight. I was being a baby, myself."

"You're not a baby. You're a beautiful woman. And I do like the idea of us setting a wedding date."

"Really?" she brightened up instantly. "You're not doing it just to please me?"

"I'm doing it to please both you and me." was his answer.

"Want to see me naked?" she asked.

"Yes," and she knew he'd say that.

"Right now?"

"Right now would be an excellent time."

She promptly walked over to a chair, unzipped the back of her dress, slipped it off, folded it and placed it on the chair.

"Bra and panties, too?" she asked.

"Yes, them too," he said.

She slipped off her bra and tossed it on the chair. Leaned over and pulled off her panties and tossed it on the chair, too. Then she came and stood in front of him with her arms down with her hands to the side not touching her hips.

"You look so beautiful in the nude," he told her.

She turned red all the way down to her knees. And he could tell for sure, of course, since he could see bare skin all the way down to her ankles. She had on a pair of high heel shoes, beige in color that was held on by two thin straps. Those shoes had drawn complements from him in the past. They didn't cover up her feet and she had beautiful feet.

"Want me to turn around?" she asked.

"Yes," he said. She knew he'd say nothing but yes to any question she asked at a time like now. She just enjoyed asking. She whirled around with her back to him to show him the back of her body. Just as beautiful from the back view as the front. It was a really fine bottom.

"You are beautiful from head to foot," he said. She turned red again, this time all the way down to her ankles.

"Now turn back around," he told her. She did so. "Walk over and stand close to me." She did that, too. "Now sit on my lap," he said.

"But your arm!" she exclaimed.

"You can be careful about my arm. Sit so you can lay your head on my good shoulder." She did so. He put his arm around her and held her, holding his beautiful, nude little wife to be.

"If you're going to set us a wedding date, you'd better make it within about the next 6 weeks or so. After that I'll be well and have to return to duty."

"You mean it," she said incredulously. "I can set us a wedding date?"

"I mean it," he said. "And I'm the luckiest man in the galaxy."

So, when they went to bed that night they were engaged.

CHAPTER 28
MILITARY WEDDING

After the cast was removed, Vic continued to stay at Red's apartment but he had to report to the base medical clinic once a day for physical therapy. Had to rebuild the shrunken arm and shoulder muscles. And walking was easier. He hadn't previously taken note of how you swing your arms when you walk and how it will hurt if one of your arms or your shoulder is tender. But he kept doing better. Red flew him to the base hospital for his weekly checkups in the red saucer. She also flew him to the clinic for his daily therapy sessions. She was pretty efficient at flying it by now.

After a couple more weeks he had started jogging. Red had started working as a secretary in her father's office after he deployed on board the spacecraft carrier. She wanted something to do. So she still worked there. But she had managed a leave of absence to care for Vic until he recovered. In fact, she explained that the only reason the medical officer gave her permission to take him home as early as she did was because she planned to stay at home and nurse her man in person.

Vic stayed busy for half a day just with his physical therapy and jogging and he had added calisthenics to his regimen. So he was busy until after noon. She'd come by and pick him up at the clinic after his physical therapy session and fly to a nearby park. She wore her jogging clothes and went jogging and did all his exercises with him. She said that she needed more exercise, too. Then they would go some place for lunch. When afternoon came he was tired enough to be ready to just relax. In fact he'd usually grab a nap in the afternoons. While he was resting Red would take care of household chores and go shopping and such.

The big day started getting closer.

When the wedding day finally arrived, Vic showed up at the church on time as any military man could be expected to do in his dinner dress uniform with tails, bow tie and shoes that shined so that you could see them a mile off. He found himself waiting at the altar when the wedding march finally began. Then he looked over his shoulder to see Red hanging onto her father's arm marching down the aisle in step with her father. He'd never seen the Admiral look so stately in his full formal dress uniform. He even carried a ceremonial light saber. Red was dressed all in white, of course, with her hair done up on top of her head. And she looked simply radiant. Vic had never seen anything so beautiful before.

They didn't have a best man or maid of honor. They were sometimes part of a wedding party but were optional. And for some reason, the most formal military weddings were the ones in which they were least likely to be part of the wedding party. But all Vic's best buddies were deployed in space, and he didn't want someone he didn't know well as part of the wedding party anyway.

Red and the Admiral finally reached the alter and the Admiral helped his daughter up the steps and placed her beside Vic. She took Vic's arm and faced forward at which time so did Vic. This is what we're fighting for, Vic thought, as the Fleet Chaplain started the ceremony. And well worth fighting for, too. And living for too, for that matter. He couldn't ever remember being so happy.

After the Chaplain completed the ceremony, Vic and Red turned and made their way back down the aisle. They walked slowly, keeping in step in time to the music, in accordance with custom. When they had gone about three steps the crowd started cheering. They continued cheering until they got out the door. Vic managed to keep his face straight but at the front door he glanced at Red and she was blushing really good. She blushed very easily. But blushing always just made her more beautiful.

After the reception, they changed to casual clothes, loaded their luggage into Vic's personal saucer and took off for Gorienth, a continent on the far side of the planet but a place very popular with tourist. Vic flew the saucer this time. His arm and shoulder were still weaker than before, but he could handle their little ship, okay. He landed on the roof of a hotel that he had picked out from his travel brochures two weeks before. A porter was there to meet them and take their luggage.

It was late so they grabbed a shower and turned in. When morning came Vic was up before Red. He was about to walk out the door when she roused up.

"Where are you going?" she asked.

"Down to grab some hot tea," he explained. "I'm accustomed to getting up early, as you already know."

"Okay, but wait for me," she replied.

"Okay," he said, and took a seat. He visited with her while she got ready. Then they went down for breakfast. Vic didn't like having breakfast in bed. He'd just rather go to the dining room to eat. Two hours later they were out by the pool just relaxing. The second day of their honeymoon, Vic wanted to go jogging. Red donned shorts and jersey and went with him. She kept up with him with no problem. Or maybe we should say he kept up with her. He was recovering from wounds and she wasn't. She'd been jogging with him for a couple of weeks. She was getting in better physical condition, too. And she decided that would be good, since she was planning a baby.

After two weeks, it was time to return to Seaside, to the Fleet Headquarters base. He reported in to the medical officer and was declared fit for light duty. The doc still didn't want him flying because he hadn't fully regained the strength in his shoulder but he was fully well otherwise.

So Vic got orders to pilot training ground school as a lecturer. He lectured the new pilot recruits on fighter tactics.

CHAPTER 29
IN A FAMILY WAY

Vic enjoyed the change of pace. He liked talking about fighter tactics to the eager new faces in his class room. Of course, just lecturing was no strain, but he found he wasn't accustomed to being on his feet all day. So his legs would be worn out before the day was over. He had just one class after another all day long. An hour for lunch, of course, but other than that he was teaching continuously.

He continued to work out each day when he got off duty. He was actually able to do a few pushups each day by now. When his shoulder started hurting, he just stopped and decided that was enough for that day.

Vic decided it was time to get Red pregnant. He decided not to just wait for nature to take its course like you'd normally do in such cases. He made his own project out of it. One night shortly after he and Red had gone to bed, he felt her flinch.

"What happened? he asked in a gentle voice.

"I just felt a glitch. Right there." She pointed to where her ovary was located.

"All right," was all that Vic said. But he removed her nightie and then slipped off her panties. He started stroking her legs and back and bottom and kissing her neck and shoulders.

She just said, "Umpf," in a kittenish tone of voice.

During sex, when he released his sperm inside her, he deliberately visualized himself inside her abdomen. He found the sperm racing up the reproductive track. He discovered that the sperm leading the pack was a sperm with the male characteristic. But not too far behind was a sperm with a female characteristic. He got inside the sperm with the female characteristic and started swimming for all he was worth. He found himself gaining on the lead sperm. And he decided it was neat being a sperm. Just like a large fish. Well, not a large fish, because he knew that sperm were microscopic in size, but he seemed large now from his perspective inside the sperm.

He kept on gaining until he was abreast with the lead sperm. The lead sperm obviously sensed that someone had overtaken him because he started swimming even more vigorously. Vic pulled ahead of him anyway. He saw the large spherical object just ahead of them. Vic managed to bang into the egg first and penetrated through the shell. The sperm that had held the lead up till then hit a fraction of a second after he did. Then a dozen or more hit the shell immediately afterward. But the zygote was already formed, and Vic now knew that it would be a girl.

Vic resumed his own beingness and looked down at Red's face resting on her pillow in the dim light. She was already sleeping peacefully. She had a blissful look on her face. She wouldn't know she was pregnant till morning. Vic just placed his cheek against her forehead and drifted off to sleep himself.

The next morning when they woke, Vic saw a look on her face he had never seen before. And he'd seen the afterglow from sex on her face countless times but he'd never seen this look on her face before. It was a look of profound contentment that made you want to stop whatever you were doing and get her anything she wanted. He'd never seen her so beautiful.

"Good morning," he said as he reached down for a kiss. She kissed him back and he said, "How are you doing?"

"Wonderful," she replied. After a short pause, she continued, "I feel wonderful all over. I don't understand it. I've never felt this way before."

"You sure are looking beautiful," he said. "And more so than usual. You've always been beautiful. But right now you'd light up the room even if it was dark."

She blushed slightly like she always did when he drew her attention to her beauty. "Do you think I'm pregnant?" she asked.

He just leaned his head down and kissed her again and gave her a squeeze. His good arm was still around her as it was when they first woke up.

* * *

Vic was in a daze when he reported to work that morning. He was so happy about being an expectant father. But he was in for a surprise. He found out he had orders to report to transport spacecraft transition school. Now, what is this? he thought. I'm a fighter pilot, not a truck driver. He wondered if he had done something wrong or if someone upstairs thought there was a permanent impairment to his shoulder to prevent him from handling fighter craft skillfully enough.

He decided it was a big enough deal to call the detailer. It was something career officers could do. It took 5 tries but he finally got through.

"Lieutenant Smith speaking," he heard over the phone.

"Ensign Mabry," he said.

"How can I help you."

"I've just been assigned to transition school to transport spacecraft. And I'm a fighter pilot, sir."

"Yes, you and about 50 other fighter pilots. The need for transport pilots has increased dramatically in the past few weeks."

"Oh." So he wasn't the only one.

"I was afraid it might have something to do with my recent injury."

"That, too. You'd be grounded for another two months before you could go to a fighter squadron. But it would be safe for you to fly transports, now."

Vic hadn't thought of that either

"You'll still be eligible for assignment to a fighter squadron again later. You're most needed as a transport pilot now."

Vic felt better after talking to the detailer. So there must be a big need for transport pilots. And he wasn't sure how his arm and shoulder would hold up in a dog fight right now anyway.

So Vic briefed his relief at the ground school and then got ready to depart for the transport school. It was on the opposite side of the continent. When Red got the news, she was excited. While she didn't like the thought of his leaving, she was glad he'd no longer be flying fighters. She thought transports would be safer.

Vic checked and found out it would be permissible to bring his blushing bride with him to his new duty station, so Vic and Red packed up and got ready to move to Ocean Beach, the city where the transport school was located. They found a small apartment near the beach. It made it convenient when they wanted to go for a swim or just sun bathe.

CHAPTER 30
BEN AND LISA

Ben and his regiment went through several more exercises. Some of them took place in desert country. Sometimes they'd make a jump over mountains. In some cases they'd make their jump over a mocked up town. But one thing was always the same. They always deployed from landing craft out of a spacecraft carrier or troop transport ship in outer space. After a year had passed since Ben had last been on leave he had another 30 days worth accrued. Their task group returned from deployment and the officers and men were allowed to go on leave if they wished. They had to stagger the time schedule. They couldn't all go on leave at once. One third of the officers and men were allowed to go on leave at the same time.

Ben found himself in the second group. They brought the men down in a landing craft and attached them to the base as soon as the ship returned and entered orbit around the planet. A company of marines had to stay on the ship and were relieved every month. But Ben had orders to take his platoon down to Seaside and get them quarters in the barracks. For a month they just stood their turn at guard duty and mainly just rested up.

Ben had stayed in touch with Lisa since he'd seen her. He'd send her a message disk every few days. She always answered it. She looked so beautiful on the view screen of his message recorder/player. She always did her hair and put on makeup before making him a message disk, but he didn't know that, of course. He had notified her he was going on leave and had told her when. He asked if she could take leave at the same time. She put in a leave request and it was approved. So they both had 30 days leave starting at the same time!

The morning she was scheduled to arrive at the space port, he checked out on leave with the base duty officer. Then he headed over to the space port to pick up Lisa.

He watched her as she walked down the ramp from the passenger ship. When she reached him he put his arms around her and gave her a big hug and kiss. Her hands were full of luggage so she couldn't hug him back but she returned his kiss with enthusiasm.

He took her bags and they went to the baggage reclaim area to get the rest of her luggage. When the luggage came down the conveyer belt, they loaded her luggage onto a cart. They rolled the cart out to a rented gravity car and Ben loaded it in the back. Then they got in the front and Ben took off. He took her to a hotel at the foot of the mountains. He landed the car and took her luggage in. He handed her a key and then showed her his key. He wanted to communicate to her that he had gotten her a separate room.

He figured she'd want to freshen up. It was about time for lunch. So he went down to the lounge and waited for her to come down. When she came down the stairs she was wearing a green miniskirt with green high heel shoes. She looked terrific.

"You are the most beautiful woman I've ever seen," he said.

She blushed before she replied, "I'll bet you tell that to all the lady marines."

"I used to," he answered. "But not since I met you. I haven't actually seen a lady marine since I met you, either. Not until now."

"Got yourself covered, don't you," she said with a wry smile, but tilted her head back for a kiss. He responded by giving her a hug *and* a kiss.

"Ready to go to lunch?" he asked.

"If you are," was her answer.

They went to the dining room for lunch. While they were eating he asked her what she wanted to do during the next 30 days or so.

"I don't know," she said. "I thought you would have planned something. Taking leave right now was your idea." So she was going to be secretive about her own wishes. He guessed she was going to see if he could figure out something she'd enjoy.

"One idea I have is to spend a couple of days on an island out in the Big Lake. We can fish or go surfing if the surf gets up."

"I like that idea," she answered with obvious interest on her face.

After lunch they went back upstairs. He walked her to her room and gave her a peck on the mouth. He looked at her and could see the droopiness in her eye lids. "Want to catch up on your sleep?"

"I don't know. What are you gonna do?" She acted suspicious.

"I have some shopping to do. I want to buy some camping supplies. If you want to catch up on your rest, you can. If you want to come shopping with me, you can do that. Just tell me what you want to do."

She relaxed then. She'd only seen him that one time before. And she had sacked out with him that time. It was the influence of the alcohol and it really surprised her when she received a message disk from him. She didn't think she'd ever see him again. But he was going slow now. They had two separate rooms. He wasn't assuming anything. She almost couldn't believe it. She had kind of regretted her decision to join him on leave but she did very much want to see him again and this was a way to achieve it. But she felt much more comfortable now.

So he went down to the rented ground car and went over to a sporting goods store. He had six months back pay in his pocket. So he had plenty of money. And he needed some camping and climbing supplies. He bought two sleeping bags, two back packs, a camping stove that would fit in one of the back packs and climbing gear. He took his purchases out to the car and climbed in. He flew back to the hotel. He left the gear in the car. They'd need food supplies but he could buy them later.

He had told Lisa that he'd wait for her in the lounge until she woke up and came down. He pulled up a map of the Big Lake from his storage disk and found an island that he thought would be a likely place to spend a couple of days. Then he went to his room, shaved and brushed his teeth. He grabbed a shower. Then he got dressed again. He went back down to the lounge and sat down to wait for Lisa.

When Lisa came down he suggested they go to dinner and dancing. That sounded fine to her.

The next day, they loaded up in Ben's rental air car and flew out to the island that Ben had picked out. They put on their swim suits and doped up with sun screen. There were lots of people there. So it was obviously a popular tourist trap. Then Ben thought he recognized someone about 50 yards or so down the beach. So after they finished setting out their lawn chairs and umbrella, he took Lisa with him and walked out down to where he had seen the familiar face. Sure enough.

It was Vic and Red. They walked on up and Ben shook Vic's hand vigorously, gave Red and hug and then introduced Lisa to them. Then Ben saw the wedding ring on Red's finger.

"Hey, congratulations! I didn't know you were getting married!" said Ben.

"Well, yeah. I haven't seen you in months, so I couldn't tell you," was Vic's reply.

"Well, it's really good to see you, and it's good to see you doing this well. Lisa and I managed a 30 day leave ourselves."

"I'm really glad you're doing that well, too." Vic invited them to join them so Ben and Lisa went back down to Ben's camp and moved all his stuff over to Vic's spot and set them up again. They had a lot of things to talk about.

After a few hours they had sort of talked themselves out. Then they decided to go for a swim. So they swam and splashed and laughed and waded around and swam and splashed and laughed some more. Then they came back to camp and started cooking steaks. There weren't any trees or firewood anywhere around but there was a marina nearby where they could buy firewood. They had steaks and potato salad with Old Red to drink.

Vic and Red had a tent. They had planned to spend the night. Ben explained how they didn't bring along a tent but he had two sleeping bags in his air car. So he walked over to the air car and retrieved the two sleeping bags. He unrolled Lisa's sleeping bag, first. Then he moved about 20 feet away and unrolled his sleeping bag. He and Lisa slept under the stars.

The next morning when they got up their first thought was breakfast, of course. Red and Lisa fixed breakfast while the men talked. After breakfast, Vic and Ben were knee deep in a conversation pertaining to space tactics. Lisa suggested to Red that they go for a swim.

It was the middle of the afternoon before Vic and Red decided they'd better head back. Vic had to start ground school for the new spacecraft he'd be flying first thing the following morning. So Vic and Red loaded up in his red flying saucer and they took off for home. Ben and Lisa decided to stay one more night and head back in the morning.

CHAPTER 31
CAMPING TRIP

The next morning they loaded up and Ben flew them to the mountain range that bordered Sea Side. He landed at the foot hills of the mountains. They took out their back packs with their climbing gear and camping supplies and started up the mountain. They made it to the first ledge. Then Lisa waited while Ben climbed up to the next ledge. Then he lowered his rope and she fastened their back packs onto his rope and he pulled them up. Then he lowered the rope again and she started walking up the precipice, pulling on the rope overhand as she went. All Fleet marines were trained in technical climbing, including women marines. She could have climbed up to the ledge by herself but it was accepted practice for the first climber to climb up using cracks in the rocks and pieces of rock jutting out and then let the next climber just walk up, holding her feet against the rocky face with the rope as she went. It was more efficient.

They made it to the top of the ridge by night fall and found a likely place to camp. They set up camp. Ben had brought along two pup tents, one for her and one for himself. So he set up the pup tents and then started a camp fire. They had to make a dry camp since they weren't near a creek or spring. They boiled water for their dry field rations and had dinner. Then Ben took out his mouth organ and played music for her. After a few songs she started singing. After a few more songs, Ben went to his back pack and got out his uke. Then he started playing again and he sang, too. Lisa changed to the harmony. They sang until the moon was high.

All this time and Ben hadn't touched her. Other than to hug and kiss her, which didn't seem like an impropriety. On her flight to Ultaria, she almost regretted her decision to come. If Ben just wanted a steady lay for a month, she wasn't it! But she was *so* lonely. Living a life in a regiment made up only of women wasn't what it was cracked up to be. So she had agreed to come and here she was. And she felt wonderful. The night was cool and the music was so very invigorating. She had a look of adoration on her face every time she looked at Ben.

And here she had a pup tent to herself. Ben must be wanting a woman. He had been deployed for over six months, himself. Then Ben put up his instrument and took Lisa by the hand. He led her to her pup tent and kissed her good night. Then he went to his pup tent and leaned down to climb in. He rolled up in his blankets to go to sleep.

In 10 minutes, he felt, rather that heard the tent flap opening. He felt the blankets pulled back and a soft tender female body slide in beside him. She just held her body up against him and said, "Thank you."

He knew what she was thanking him for. She was thanking him for not rushing her. He'd have gone the entire 30 days without touching her if there was any risk at all of it rubbing her wrong, and she had finally figured it out.

Lisa was just a little bundle of heaven.

* * *

The next morning they broke camp and resume their hike. They repelled down the opposite side of the mountain. They found a creek to refill their canteens. They continued their hike till noon. Then they stopped and built a fire to boil water for their rations again. The trees and grass were beautiful. And there were wild flowers in bloom. Ben looked at Lisa. She looked beautiful. She had a flush on her face. It was obvious she was happy.

After lunch they shouldered their packs and started out again. By the middle of the afternoon, Lisa started looking tired. So Ben found a place to make camp, this time near a creek.

After they'd pitched camp and got a camp fire started, Lisa said, "I want to visit my father."

"I'd like to meet your father," was Ben's reply. "Where does he live?"

"He lives in Seaside," she answered. "He was at a school in Dolton, when I first landed in Seaside. He had to go to school for a week to get up to date on a product his company is going to manufacture. But he should be home tomorrow."

"We can head back to Seaside anytime you wish," he told her.

So the next morning they reversed their direction and climbed back up the mountain, repelled down the west side of it and made plans to visit Lisa's father.

He sensed somehow that she wanted to be alone when she was reunited with her father. So he waited until she called her father to see when he'd be home. Then he found a taxi and put all her luggage in the back and paid the taxi driver in advance. He got her father's address from her and made a date with her for the following afternoon at 2 PM to go work out in the gym.

Then Ben turned in the gravity car and rented a gravity cycle. It was like a motor cycle except without wheels. It traveled about six feet off the ground usually but you could go as high as 500 feet if you wished. Then he went back to his hotel room.

The following afternoon he drove the gravity cycle over and picked her up at 2 PM. She climbed on the back of the gravity cycle and he took her to the gym. Parking was in the back of the building. They went inside and rotated through the various exercise machines. Fleet marines like to stay in shape, even the female ones. So they went to the gym and did their jogging to warm up. Then they rotated through all the different weight lifting machines. After they were both hot and sweaty and puffing good, they went to their respective dressing rooms and changed into swim suits so they could go spend some time in the sauna. They were already sweaty. They really did sweat good once they were inside the hot box. And Lisa looked terrific in her bikini.

After a shower and getting changed back to street clothes they went back out to Ben's gravity cycle and he took her back to her father's home where he dropped her off. She invited him over for dinner so he could meet her father. So he went back to the hotel room to change and wait until evening.

He showed up at 7 o'clock on time and knocked on the door. Lisa came and let him in. She introduced him to her father. He was a gray headed gentleman, slender and about Ben's height. He shook hands with him and seemed glad to meet him. He was eager to meet a man that could make that kind of impression on his daughter.

During dinner, Ben found out that Jeb Mann was an engineer for a company that made parts for space ships. He was talkative and Ben was a good listener. They had a very pleasant evening.

CHAPTER 32
SURVIVING

When morning came, Jules and Nina got up and Jules got the fire to going again. He still had to decide what to do with her. He started to make breakfast by getting some flour out of his backpack. He poured some of it in a bowl and reached into his backpack and got out some other ingredients. Nina reached over and took the bowl away from him and started mixing the ingredients herself. She stirred it, added water and made up some kind of dough. She rolled her hands in flour, then took the dough and pulled off pieces of it, rolled it into little balls, then mashed each one into a flat disk. She found a flat pan that would fit over the frying pan. She put the biscuits in the frying pan and covered it with the other pan. She took a stick and raked some coals from the fire. She placed the frying pan over the coals and then scooped up some more coals with a flat rock she found. She put them on top of the covering pan. She hadn't seen Jules make biscuits any way except by frying them. So with her makeshift Dutch oven she could find out how he liked baked biscuits.

Then she looked around and found Jules gone. She jumped up in alarm at first. She looked around. His blankets were still lying on the ground. He had rolled them up and just left them there. Did he abandon her? Why would he do that now? Why didn't he just leave last night if he was going to do that?

For now she was hungry. She decided she was going to finish breakfast and eat. Before the biscuits were done Jules showed up with a small animal he had shot. He skinned it skillfully, stuck a sharp stick through it and arranged it over the fire to broil. And he also took a pot, filled it with water from his canteen and placed it on the fire.

Nina hadn't heard a shot. So how could he kill an animal? She didn't notice the crossbow slung over his shoulder until he removed it to sit down on a log. In a few minutes they had two cups of hot brew ready and nibbled on hot biscuits and sipped tea while waiting for the meat to broil. Jules took some salt from a sack and sprinkled it on the broiling meat periodically.

Nina hadn't had a decent meal in weeks. After the meat was done, she dug in and ate with an appetite. Jules ate several biscuits. He didn't say anything about them and Nina watched him. She was hoping he liked them but her only clue was that he kept reaching for another after finishing one.

After they had finished breakfast, they broke camp and Jules led off into the woods again along a mountain trail. Nina tried to keep up but the trails went up and down, up and down. They were skirting a mountain. She finally had to stop and catch her breath. When Jules was 50 yards or so ahead of her, he stopped, turned around and waited for her to catch up. He never said a word. Then when she finally recovered her breath enough so that she could continue, he turned and resumed their trek. How can I possibly keep up with a mountain goat? she thought.

By noon she was exhausted. Jules didn't seem to notice. He stopped and built a fire to cook their noon meal. After they had eaten she went to sleep. When she woke up several hours later Jules was gone again! She felt panicky at first. Then she remembered he had done this before. And he always returned. She decided she would try to see if she could please him by having dinner ready by the time he returned. She set out to make a campfire like she had seen Jules do. He had left his backpack at their camp. So he would definitely return!

When Jules returned before nightfall she had a pot of boiled jerky and beans cooked and a pan of biscuits that she thought he liked since he ate them. She had also made a pan of gravy this time.

He sat down on a rock and said, "There will be another ship soon. I can't say exactly when. But another group is forming. You can join them."

The following day they were moving down a mountain trail. Nina was sore all over but she was keeping up with Jules better than she had at first. He didn't have to stop and wait for her to catch up as often. They stopped at noon to make camp and cook their noon meal. After they had eaten, Jules said, "I need to do some scouting. You should be safe here until I return." He normally never told her he was leaving. He normally just disappeared. He got up and walked on off into the trees.

Nina decided to gather up the pots and pans and take them to the nearby creek and wash them. She rinsed off each skillet and baking pan, then scrubbed it with sand then rinsed it again. She had finished and gathered up all the pans, plates, cups and all and was walking back to the fire when she heard footsteps. She knew it couldn't be Jules because he never made a sound while walking. Then she saw a man in an Imperial uniform. She froze in a state of panic at first.

Then she heard him say in Armenian, "What is this?" He was tall and lanky and was wearing a regulation helmet and had a blast rifle over his shoulder. He had an evil look on his face but was clean shaven. Nina saw another soldier behind him and another behind him. She didn't know how many they were but immediately dropped the pots and pans she was holding and started running. The Imperial soldier was quick as a cat. He caught her in a half a dozen steps. He shoved her to the ground and immediately started undoing her pants. The other soldier came and started to help. She started hitting the first soldier with both her hands as fast as she could, though rather ineffectively. The second soldier went around behind her and grabbed her hands. The first soldier who appeared to be in charge grabbed the waist of her pants and ripped them loose on one side. Then he ripped the other side loose. They came off in ribbons of cloth. Then he grabbed her panties and ripped them first on one side, then the other. Her legs were still free so she started kicking him. Two other soldiers appeared out of thin air and grabbed her legs and pulled them apart.

She managed to get her hands free and raked the Squad Leader's face viciously with her nails. The soldier that was holding her hands got another grip. Then she heard a "zip" and the soldier lying on top of her collapsed, his body limp as a rag.

Within another second she heard another "zip" and felt hot blood spurt onto her face. The soldier that had been holding her hands collapsed, his face falling on her face, blood still gushing. She could see what looked like a short arrow protruding from his throat. The two soldiers that were holding her legs turned loose, got up and started running. Nina heard a "splat" and saw an arrow appear in the middle of the back of one of them. The other kept running. He ran down the trail around a bend so he was obscured by brush. Nina struggled to get up. Then she heard another "splat." Then silence.

It was probably 5 minutes when Jules appeared holding a crossbow with a loaded bolt. He said nothing but immediately started gathering up the pots and pans and placing them in his backpack which he had left behind. He tied his blankets to the top of it and put it on his back. He grabbed Nina's backpack and handed it to her. She put it on quickly and Jules rushed down toward the creek and ran downstream 50 yards or so and then waded out into the water and crossed the stream. Nina followed him and sucked in her breath at the icy cold of the stream.

Nina was naked from the waist down except when she stood up her buttocks were barely covered by her shirt tail. There was no trail, Jules just struck out through the brush. Nina could not move silently through brush as could Jules and she had no protection from briars on bushes. Her legs were scratched and cut and were bleeding before they got through the thickest of the brush. They did finally come to a trail and Jules rushed up the trail with Nina struggling to keep up.

When they reached another creek, Jules stepped down into the water and just followed the creek upstream for several hundred yards. Nina's legs and feet were numb by this time and she left a blood trail from her bleeding legs in the stream, though it dissipated quickly. The cold did seem to stop the bleeding faster.

Then Jules left the creek, reversed direction and started along a trail that followed the creek bank for a few hundred yards and then he left the trail and walked along some solid grass turf that didn't leave a trail. He walked up past a hill with a steep bank, went around a corner and then pulled some branches back to reveal a cave. He walked inside and Nina followed. He picked up a candle, lit it and placed it on a ledge in the wall. He lit another candle and placed it on another ledge in the opposite wall. She saw that blankets had been spread along the right wall.

"Lie down," he instructed. She did so. He pulled the blankets over her covering her shivering legs and sat down at her feet and started removing her boots. After he had her boots off, he unbuttoned his shirt and placed her feet against his belly, holding his hands against her insteps.

When feeling first started returning to her feet, she felt a tingling sensation, and then they started to hurt. The part of his belly that her feet were touching was like ice by then. He moved her feet a little wider apart so they could find a warm area of his belly to rest against. In a few minutes her feet were warm.

Then he rummaged in his backpack and found a first aid kit. He found some adhesive tape. He pulled back the blanket and started taping the cuts and scratches on her legs. He pulled her legs apart and took a flashlight from his pocket and shined it on her vulva and inspected it for injuries. None. So they apparently didn't achieve their purpose. He wrapped the blankets around her legs and tucked her in.

"I'm thirsty," she said. He reached over and picked up a canteen and handed it to her so she could drink. She felt warm and drowsy. Within minutes she was asleep.

CHAPTER 33
TRANSPORT TRAINING

Vic found out that the transport spacecraft were larger than strike spacecraft but smaller than patrol ships. And he learned that they took off from their belly rather than taking off from their tail as fighter craft did. That was necessary to avoid jumbling up their cargo any more than necessary.

And he learned that former fighter pilots had 3 times as much life expectancy as pilots that started flying transports with no previous fighter experience. So that was one of the reasons he was chosen to fly transports. Supplies were being shipped from one planet to another on a much larger scale than usual. So something was in the wind, though Vic knew no one would tell him what it was.

The transport craft was easy to fly, he found out, after he had completed ground school and started flying. Their training included everything except acrobatic flight, of course. They still had to master instrument flying and formation flying.

And he appreciated the extra time that he had with Red. When he got time off they went to the beach often. They went swimming or surfing or fishing. Both of them managed a good tan before Vic's training was completed.

Vic went out to the launching pad to man up for a training flight. Steve was going to be his co-pilot today. When Vic walked up to the spacecraft, he had already started his preflight procedures. Dan would be the navigator. Steve and Vic took turns flying pilot and copilot so they could get used to flying in either seat. Dan flew as navigator every time. He had been trained as a pilot initially and flew scouting spacecraft for a few months but when he was transferred to transports he had decided to specialize just in navigation. He had a mathematical bent.

Vic remembered Dan from his own fighter pilot days, of course. He had blond, wavy hair, was blue-eyed and well built. He was a little taller and broader in the shoulders than Vic. Steve had freckles and red hair and was more wiry in build than either of them. He wasn't quite as tall as Vic.

They climbed into the spacecraft and went forward. Vic sat down in the pilot's seat and Steve in the copilot's seat which was on the right. Dan's navigator's station was in a compartment just aft of the flight deck.

They would have a flight engineer on long flights but didn't really need one just for routine training flights. As far as that went, Vic knew how to navigate a spacecraft. Any fighter pilot had to be his own navigator since he flew a single-piloted spacecraft. But the navigators needed to get their training hours up so they were included in the crew for training flights.

They completed the pre-take off checklist and Vic added power. The spacecraft left the launch pad and drifted up into the air. Vic thought it was neat to just drift up slowly. There was an anti-gravity device that reduced the gravity to zero and then made it go negative so they could increase altitude. The main drives were at idle. After they were above 100,000 feet, Vic added power so they could leave the planet. Today they were on an instrument training flight. They had to get proficient at flying on instruments. So they were going into outer space and would fly to an asteroid and then return. Vic would fly half the flight in the pilot's seat, then he and Steve would trade so Steve could get his practice at flying pilot.

While Vic was a trained navigator, he found that navigating in fighter craft was different. You normally just plotted your position in reference to the spacecraft carrier. But he now had Dan to give him headings to fly. It was all black in space though they could see the sun. It was an orange ball, enough bigger than the other stars so that it stood out. Anything else you looked at was just black goo.

"Come 3 degrees to the right, and 1 degree up," Dan called to him on the intercom. Vic said, "Roger," and made the change in heading. The gravity from a nearby asteroid had apparently pulled them off course.

When they started approaching their destination, Vic put the power in reverse thrust and started slowing down. They'd land on the asteroid so he'd get a practice landing, then he and Steve would change seats so Steve could get the practice of a take-off. Vic found a flat area to land in and brought her down slowly. When they touched the ground he knew he'd made a mistake. The ground crumbled and gave way underneath them. He immediately added power and pulled up several hundred feet above the surface. The dust that had been stirred up obscured the view completely so he couldn't see what he hit but he knew it was an underground cave that was near the surface that had caved in. So he let the spacecraft drift along looking for a better place to land.

He found a place that looked solid and set her down again. The entire spacecraft disappeared in a cloud of dust. He immediately added power and brought her up above the dusty turmoil again. This time he just brought her up to a hover above the dust and unstrapped. Steve saw what he was doing and unstrapped, too. They changed seats. It looked like they weren't going to find a solid place to land but they didn't have to land. They could change seats while in a hover.

Steve added power and left the asteroid. Dan gave him a heading to fly and he got the spacecraft headed back to their home planet.

CHAPTER 34
THE GREEN MEN

Vic completed his check-in procedure at his transport squadron and reported aboard the transport spacecraft he was assigned to. He found out he would be one of the copilots. The pilot in command was Lieutenant Commander Hal Stoddard. He noticed that Dan reported aboard, too. He would be one of the navigators. They'd have 3 navigators, one to go with each crew. The loading crew was just finishing up the loading of the cargo. Hal had the crew gather just outside the spacecraft and introduced all the other crew members to each other. Then he briefed them on the flight.

They all climbed into the spacecraft and Vic found himself in the copilot's seat going over checklists. In 30 minutes they were spaceborne and on course to their destination. Only then did Vic learn what their destination was. A new fleet base was being built on the planet Misten and they were flying construction supplies to them.

They joined up in formation with three other transports. They had fighter craft flying escort for them above, below and on both sides. So it appeared that they had the forces needed to cope with any threat from the Imperial Fleet. They continued their course toward Misten.

They arrived at Plisten, the moon of Misten in which the loading/unloading station was located. It was cratered and had rough mountains like you'd see on any moon surface. It did not have a breathable atmosphere and had light gravity, about one third as much as Ultaria. They docked their transport craft at the docking station and the dock crew unloaded their cargo. The docking station was an enclosed bubble made of transparent plastic and had breathable air inside it. The unloading was done by green men.

Vic had heard about the green men. They did not have to eat. They absorbed all their nourishment from sunlight. And they wore no clothing. They had to go nude all the time to absorb enough sunlight to subsist. But they did not look indecent. Their hair looked more like tiny pine needles than hair and it covered the loin area of their bodies. The males also had green hair on their chests and legs. So it looked as if they were clothed. While they did not have to eat they did have to drink water. And they had to have mineral water because that was their only source of minerals. They could work inside the loading dock because it was pressurized and plenty of light could come in from the dome above.

The planet Misten was populated with green men and women. There was vegetation growing in abundance on the planet but since the Mistenites did not eat, they saw no reason to farm or produce any kind of food. However, they did like to trade for goods they could buy. The green women liked trinkets and ornaments. And the men bought tools. They lived in houses and liked to build nice houses and the women decorated the interiors of their houses. While they had to maximize the time spent in the sun during the day so they'd take in enough nourishment to subsist, they preferred to sleep indoors at night. And they liked to keep pot plants as part of the interior decoration of their homes. While they could dig soil from the ground, they had no means of making the pots to put the plants in. So when the Ultarians came and wanted to build factories and give them jobs, they went to work willingly so they could earn the money to buy the things they wanted from the traders who landed on the planet periodically. Factories were built by the New Empire to manufacture the supplies, equipment and even spacecraft. The traders, of course, set up stores in all of the villages.

The women went to work alongside the men, some of them with babies they carried in belly packs. They had no means of making belly packs before. But now that fabric was available they could make a belly pack for their babies and carry them along wherever they went. There were portions of the belly pack that was made up of transparent or mesh material so sunlight could get through. They gave their babies water with baby bottles (something else that they had bought from the stores). Green women had breasts for giving their babies water, so the baby bottles weren't essential but were definitely convenient. They didn't have as much hair as the men but their loin area had enough of the green hair to keep them from looking too indecent. Their breasts had no hair. So they still presented something of a risqué appearance.

Vic learned from one of the dock workers that they did have various forms of wildlife on the planet. They had animals that grazed in the valleys and meadows and predator animals that preyed on them. They had purchased weapons from the Fleet to help defend themselves against wolves or mountain lions so they could now travel outside their villages if they wanted. With their spears and flint axes it would be very difficult to kill a bear or wolf. They had no reason to kill animals for food since they didn't eat but they needed to defend themselves against any predator creatures that might want to make a dinner of *them*.

The green people were good workers and were employed to build space ships for the New Empire. Many shipyards had been constructed at various points on the planet. At one point Vic found that the off loading was halted because they had to take a space barge to the surface to make room in the storage dock for the additional cargo yet to be off loaded. But as soon as the space barge left the dock there was more room so they then continued their off loading process. The co-pilots were responsible for supervising the off loading.

After the unloading was completed, the transport crew manned up and took off. They were spaceborne again and headed back to make another run. It took them three days to arrive back at their source point. That's why they had three crews. Each crew was on duty for eight hours, at which time they changed crews. They had bunks on the ship where they could sleep. They arrived at the source point and docked. Then the entire crew secured and went inside the facility to eat and get some sleep. They had sleeping quarters with showers and all. After a hot meal and a good night's sleep they felt greatly refreshed. Their new cargo was loaded by the time the crew was ready to go again.

CHAPTER 35
WINTER IN THE MOUNTAINS

When Nina awoke all was dark inside the cave. She felt panicky. She started to scream, then rolled over to her right and saw a flicker of light on the opposite side of the cave. Jules was lighting a candle. He had spread some blankets on the ground for himself and apparently awoke when she did. He had heard her uneven breathing when she awoke.

"Are you all right?" he asked.

"Yes," she answered. She was, now that she knew that Jules was still nearby. She got up and started walking toward the entrance of the cave. Jules got up and followed her. He pulled the pile a brush away from the entrance to the cave to reveal a solid wall of white. He poked his fist through the snow so they could see that the entire countryside was covered with a mantle of white.

"Wintertime in the mountains," he said. "You can go to the back of the cave. He knew that she needed to answer a call of nature. Her legs were already starting to get cold by the time she returned to her blankets.

"Lie back down and cover up," he told her. He went to some boxes against the wall and took out a couple of cans. He rummaged through his backpack and found a can opener. He found two plates and in a few minutes, Nina found herself eating a cold breakfast of fish, beans and crackers. He handed her the canteen so she could get a drink when she wanted.

After breakfast he told her to stand up. She obeyed without thinking to ask why. He took a piece of string and measured her from waist to ankle. Then he measured her around the waist. Then he tied a knot in the string. Then he moved it down to the middle of her buttocks and measured again. Then he measured her thigh and calf. She was full of curiosity by then but somehow it didn't seem appropriate to ask what he was doing. She'd find out anyway, she decided as she watched Jules rummage through some cured animal skins.

Jules found several skins, checked the length, then he pulled his measuring string across one of them, took a piece of charcoal and marked it. He held the string across the other end and marked it. He placed several marks between them. Then he drew a line from the mark at one end to the other following the marks in between. He marked it on both sides, then he pulled some scissors out of one of the boxes resting against the wall and starting cutting the skin. So they must be leather scissors, Nina thought.

He found a tool for punching holes, got a needle and some thick thread and started sewing. She just huddled in her blankets to stay warm and watched him work in the dim light. It was ten minutes or so before she figured out he was making her a pair a leather pants! She definitely needed new pants since her pants had been ripped to shreds by the Imperial soldiers.

It took an hour or two for him to finish his handiwork. He handed them to her. He didn't look away when she pulled back the blankets to put them on. They fit snug, like Jules's pants did so they wouldn't snag on brush. There were seams up the sides. She pulled them up to her waist to find there was a tongue in the middle and laces she could tighten that went from the crotch to the waist. She drew them up tight and tied a bow knot. They fit perfectly.

"Thank you," she said and without thinking reached over and gave him a hug. He put his arms around her and gave her a light squeeze but then he stepped back. She released him and said, "I'm sorry."

"It's okay," he answered. "You had to have you some clothes to stay warm." Then he sat down and she did likewise.

She took time to put on her boots. She noticed that Jules had his moccasins on. He must have slept in his leather pants and moccasins both.

"What is that?" she motioned to a place near the mouth of the cave that was indented from the wall.

"My fireplace. I have a flue built that will take the smoke out through the top of the cave so the cave won't fill with smoke."

"Can we light the fire?" she then asked.

"No. The Imperial troops might still be looking for us. If there is a patrol nearby they'd smell the smoke and it would lead them right to us. We have to stay holed up here for several weeks until they finally give up on finding us, though the snow will help. The Imperial troops don't move around nearly as much in the winter time as they do during the summer. But I have to make sure you make it on the next smuggler ship that leaves."

A look of dark depression came over her face. She knew she had to get off the planet but the thought of leaving Jules was something that she hadn't even thought of before. She sat stunned now that the idea had time to take effect.

CHAPTER 36
FORCED LANDING

They went back out and manned up their spacecraft and headed up into space again. After about 4 hours, Vic saw unknown blips on his radar screen. It became obvious within minutes that they were being attacked. The fighter craft on their right found themselves very heavily engaged with enemy fighters. Then the right turret gunner on his own transport craft was firing.

Hal was doing some light jinking when he saw an enemy fighter coming directly toward them. He had to settle out and fly straight to give the gunners a stable platform to shoot from, too. So he worked on taking evasion action as much as he could without any violent changes in course or speed. This way, variations in speed seemed to have the least effect on the gunners but it still made it possible to avoid a lot of the laser torpedoes directed toward them.

Then wham! They were hit. Hal tried to continue to take evasive action but found out that their drives were damaged. Hal told Vic to put in an emergency call to the flight leader. He tried only to find out that the communications equipment had been knocked out. Dan had to navigate manually when he found out that the electronic navigational equipment was not operational, but that was something he was good at. So he located the nearest habitable planet to land on and gave Hal a heading to fly towards it. The battle raged behind them between the friendly and enemy fighters but the only thing for them to do was try to save their ship and crew. They approached the planet's atmosphere and Hal managed to maneuver over a continent. It would be better than landing in the ocean, of course. It was a planet with a life support system suitable to human life.

He couldn't maneuver into orbit but he had some control over their gravity drives so he could control their rate of descent, at least. He managed to make a forced landing into a grassy area. He hit the ground harder than he wanted to but at least he got her down.

They completed the shut down check list and one of the crewmen in the back opened the hatch and lowered the ladder. They climbed down the ladder to see a flat grassy plain all around them. There wasn't a cloud in the sky and the sun was shining brightly. It was warm with almost no wind. The terrain was flat all the way to the horizon in all directions except Vic could see a purple mountain range off in the distance when he looked to the northeast.

* * *

"Get all your survival gear together and get them loaded into your back packs," Hal told them. "We can't stay here. We have to find a place where we have water before we can make a camp. And Vic, get out your belt radio and turn it on to receive."

Vic did so. It had a test button you could push to see if it was operational. It wasn't. Hal saw it, so he got out his own belt radio and tested it. It didn't work either. They found out it was true for the entire crew.

"It looks like whatever knocked out our ship's radio burned out all our personal radios as well," Hal concluded.

They saw what looked like a mountain in the far distance. Hal guessed that mountains meant mountain streams and mountain streams meant water. So they took the water they had and divided it up among the canteens of all the men, shouldered their packs and started out toward the mountain in the distance.

By looking at the sun, Vic could tell it was about mid morning on this planet. It wasn't long before it started to get hot. Vic felt the sweat pouring off his forehead. And none of them were accustomed to doing very much walking. Vic was grateful for the jogging he had done while recovering from his wounds. He knew that gave him more endurance. But his left arm and shoulder started hurting almost right away. The back pack irritated them. Vic decided he was going to have to settle down to a miserable day. As they walked they saw some four footed creatures in the distance grazing.

When the sun was overhead, they stopped to rest and have a meal of their emergency rations. They removed their back packs and most of them just sat on them. But Vic was glad to finally be able remove his back pack.

They had a paleographer in the crew named Jacob. "This planet has just barely started its industrial revolution," he explained. "A lot of the continents are populated with mainly herders and planters. But they have railroads. And some of the continents are somewhat industrialized and have factories to manufacture tools and equipment. It looks like this is a herder area from the cattle we've seen.

"And cattle also have to have water. If we find a cattle trail, we could probably follow it and find some kind of water hole."

"But we haven't come to a cattle trail," Hal observed.

"This is very arid country," Jacob explained. "The water holes will be few and far between and, of course, there won't be near as many cattle in any given area, either. But if we keep walking we should come to a cattle trail, eventually."

After they had their meal of emergency rations and had taken a couple of swigs of water from their canteens, they shouldered their packs and started their dreary trek toward the distant mountain again. It didn't seem any closer.

In the middle of the afternoon, Vic looked over to his right to see a cloud of dust rising on the horizon. After a few minutes he looked again and saw some four legged animals running toward them. He notified Hal, who stopped the group and looked over toward them. He shaded his eyes to see better. "Yeah, and it appears they have two heads," he remarked.

"Men mounted on horseback," explained Jacob. "This is herder country and man will have domesticated horses to ride and herd their cattle."

Everyone knew about horses. There were places on their home planet where they had horses. In tourist areas, you could rent horses to ride just for pleasure.

The riders continued to run toward them. When they reached them they rode around them in such a fashion as to surround them and then held drawn rifles on them. One of them shouted something.

Their chief navigator was Bob, who was also a linguist. He knew the languages of most of the planets in this sector. "He's telling us to halt," Bob explained.

Another one of the riders said something. "They say we are

dressed kind of funny," Bob translated. Another of the riders said something and he said, "And they wonder why we're afoot."

Hal said, "Ask them why the rifles."

Bob did so. The man who seemed to be the leader of the group answered. Bob said, "He thinks we might be rustlers."

"Ask him how we can be rustlers if we're afoot," Hal told him.

Bob did so. And when he did they seemed to relax a little. Bob went on to explain to them that they were looking for water so they could find a place to camp. He knew that aircraft hadn't been invented on this planet yet so he couldn't explain where they came from.

None of the crewmembers had thought to draw their blast pistols. Their attention was riveted on the riders. When they saw them with rifles pointed at them, it would have obviously been very unwise to make it look like they were going to start shooting.

The riders placed their rifles in saddle sheaths that were apparently provided for the purpose. The leader told them that if they'd wait here, they'd go get horses for them. He barked orders to two of his riders who rode off in the direction from which they had come.

The men on the ground didn't draw their weapons and the riders took no steps to disarm them. It appeared that their blast pistols must not have looked like weapons to the riders. They weren't in holsters. They were just fastened to their belts by spring clips.

The riders dismounted and loosened the cinches on their saddles. They hobbled their horses to let them graze. Then each cowboy got out a piece of paper and a small sack. They each opened their sack and shook out what looked like tiny dry leaves onto the paper. Then they each rolled the paper up licked it and sealed it. It appeared to be a small cylinder. Then they placed one end in their mouths, took out a match and lit it. Then they each drew a big puff of smoke and inhaled it. They exhaled with relish.

"Tobacco," Jacob explained. "It was a popular mode of entertainment at the beginning of the industrial revolution on nearly every planet."

Vic thought the smoke really had a fragrant smell to it. He could understand why they'd enjoy burning those tiny leaves.

"It's better not to smoke, because it's habit forming," Jacob elaborated.

"What if they offer us a smoke?" one of the men asked.

"If you can't decline without being rude, then accept but don't inhale the smoke," Steve explained. "It isn't habit forming unless you inhale it."

Vic had noticed that every cowboy had inhaled the smoke of his cigarette.

After a couple of hours the two cowboys came back with horses, 15 horses, one for every man. So they mounted up and started off in the direction the cowboys had come from to begin with. But they moved off at a walk now. There was no reason to run the horses any more.

Vic noticed that all the riders that had rode up to them had saddles on their horses, and bridles on their horse's heads. But the horses that were brought for the crew to ride only had a saddle blanket on each horse and a rope hackamore instead of a bridle.

That wasn't so hard to understand. They might have spare horses for 15 men but not that many spare saddles.

CHAPTER 37
RANCHER

On the ride to the ranch, Vic found out very quickly that riding is harder work than walking, though keeping the horses at a walk made it easier than if they were galloping. A horse does walk faster than a man and a man doesn't expend as much energy riding a horse at a walk as he would walking himself, so in that respect it was an improvement. And he was able to fasten his backpack around his waist so it was behind him. So his arm and shoulder didn't hurt as much.

It was late evening when they rode up to the ranch buildings. A cowboy toward the front with white hair, a gray felt hat and a short white beard, dismounted and walked up to the front door of what looked like a dwelling house. He turned and said something to the riders, then knocked on the door. Then when the door opened he removed his hat.

"He said he was going to tell the boss we are here," explained Bob.

When the door opened they found out that the boss turned out to be a woman. She looked like she was under 30 years old and she wore a long dress that went almost to the ground, though they could see a pair of boots with pointed toes sticking out at the hemline. Her dress had long sleeves and a high neck. It seemed like a very modest dress but was made of nice fabric. Her black hair was piled on the top of her head.

She first greeted who was apparently the foreman of the cowboys and then looked up at the new arrivals. Then she spoke to the foreman.

"Take them to the cook shack and feed them," Bob translated for them. "And then let them bed down in the barn." She looked them over like if she was trying to see if there was someone she knew among them. And Vic noticed her eyes stopped for an instant when

143

she looked at him.

But then she went back inside and the foreman gave some orders to the men. Then he said something to the transport crew.

"He said to ride our horses over to the corral and put them inside. Chuck will be ready in a little while," Bob translated for them.

"What is chuck?" asked Hal.

"Their word for food," answered Bob.

The foreman gave some more instructions to Bob. He had figured out by now that he was their translator. "He said to put our back packs and gear in the barn. That's where we'll sleep, tonight."

So after they put their horses in the corral, they went into the barn. It was roomy and had a stack of hay at one end. They removed their back packs and laid them against the wall. Then Bob suggested that they go ahead and unroll their blankets and get their beds made while it was light. It would be harder to do in the dark.

They did so and just sat around on their blankets, waiting to be called to come and eat. They were impressed with the hospitality they were receiving. To undertake to feed 15 men was a pretty good chore in itself.

It was nice just to get to sit down again for a few minutes. They'd had a rather vigorous and busy time of it for the past 24 hours or so. They were tired. Just before they were called to go eat, a cowboy came to the barn and walked up to Vic. He said something to him that Vic didn't understand, of course. Bob told him that he said the boss wanted to see him. So Vic walked to the big house while the other men started walking over to the cook shack.

When they got up to the front of the house, the cowboy walked up the steps and knocked. The door opened but this time what he saw was a young girl, who looked like she was in her teens. She spoke to Vic in a foreign language but motioned to a chair. So he came in and sat down. The cowboy then left.

In a few minutes the boss came in. She was now dressed in an evening gown, the kind that was off the shoulder and with a plunging neckline. Her hair was freshly combed and flowing down over her shoulders. She was obviously a very beautiful woman.

"I'm glad to meet you," she said in Armenian. "My name is Myrna."

Surprised to hear her speak in a language he understood, Vic stood up. "I'm Vic," he said, also in Armenian. He didn't know what was going on, and he didn't know anyone on this planet spoke Armenian. She escorted him to the dining room with a table and two chairs arranged so the diners could face each other across the table. She motioned to one the chairs. He nodded his acknowledgement and then walked around and held her chair out for her and seated her before going around to his seat.

"You speak Armenian," was the first thing that Vic said.

"Yes," and she smiled. She had a beautiful smile. "I grew up on Armenia. My late husband was from Armenia. He came here and started this ranch. Then he went back to Armenia looking for a wife and found me. I've lived here ever since."

"Your late husband?" Vic queried.

"Yes. He was killed in our last fight with rustlers. As far as I know we've eradicated all cattle rustlers from the continent, but we had our share of losses. My husband was one of the losses. He was a very brave man and always did his part in any fighting that we had to do."

"I'm sorry to hear about it," Vic explained.

"What is past is past," she said. "That was four years ago. I still like living here. I like the wide open spaces and I enjoy this old house. And I like the peace and quiet we enjoy when we aren't having to fight rustlers or land grabbers."

The younger woman came in now bringing a bottle of some beverage. She poured a little in Vic's glass. It was obvious he was expected to sample it. He tasted it. It was delicious. Only a little sweet, but had just the kind of flavor that Vic liked. He nodded his approval and she finished filling his glass. Then she walked around and filled Myrna's glass.

She held up her glass toward Vic in some kind of gesture that he didn't understand before taking her first drink. He responded with the same gesture. So he was being treated to a gourmet meal. And the other men were eating in the cook shack. He was starting to wonder why the difference.

She kept chattering about her life here on Oltaria. And she talked of how her husband had been a spacer on a merchant trader. He had worked his way up to the rank of First Officer and then was shipwrecked on one of the moons of Oltaria. They had sent an emergency landing craft to the surface to see if they could find a place to buy supplies to keep the crew from starving while waiting to be rescued.

"The shipping company finally did send a repair ship to Jeff's wreck and the crew was rescued and the ship salvaged. But in the meantime, Jeff liked this planet. He saved his money, and then later, bought a ticket on a passenger space liner and came here and settled."

The waitress came by again and gave each one of them a tossed salad and a bottle of dressing. Everything was especially delicious. This lady did live well, he decided.

"What do you do for entertainment?" he asked.

"There is a city that is about 50 miles of so from here. They have parties and dinners, there. But I also like to just go riding and enjoy the fresh air and sunshine," she explained.

When they had finished their salads the girl, Jamie, Vic had learned her name by now, brought each of them a steak with a baked potato and all the trimmings.

"The food is excellent," Vic told her. He was sure he was expected to say that, but it was also true. "I wonder why I have been invited in here to eat with you, while the other men eat out in the cook shack with the hired men."

"Because you look just like my late husband," she replied with an admiring look on her face. "You are very handsome."

He tried not to blush. "Thank you," he said. "You are a rather unusually beautiful woman your own self."

She *did* blush at *his* comment. Then Jamie came to refill their wine glasses. By now Vic had figured out what her motives were. She was interested in him *romantically.* He was going to have to explain to her that he was married and had a wife that was expecting and try to do so in a way that wouldn't hurt her feelings. *This* was something he didn't know he was going to have to deal with.

They had finished their steaks. After another glass of wine the girl brought them dessert, some kind of fruit cobbler. And it was delicious, too, as everything was. He decided he could give her some background on himself, now. She'd done a pretty good job of filling him in on her life and her goals.

"We have a war going on in outer space," he explained. "Our ship was battle damaged and we had to make a force landing on your planet."

"I'm not surprised. The Empire is always at war with someone. I understand they have a pretty big rebellion with the planet Ultaria they're having to put down."

"It's grown beyond the point of rebellion. Ultaria has organized a confederation of planets of her own and continues to grow. We're up to 137 planets, now. But the Old Empire continues to fight us and keeps trying to regain what she has lost."

"Fight *us*. Are you fighting for the Rebels?"

"Yes, except we no longer call ourselves Rebels. We call ourselves the New Empire, instead."

"That makes you a turncoat!" she exclaimed. She was obviously disappointed, and seemed somewhat angry. She had correctly surmised that he was Armenian because he did not speak with a foreign accent.

"If I'm going to fight and die, I intend to fight and die *for* something I believe instead of *against* it," he explained simply.

She paused a moment to let what he said have time to soak in. So he must have been born and raised on Armenia. But then somehow he must have gotten himself commissioned in the Rebel Fleet. She recognized the officer's insignia on the collar of his flight suit. So she looked at him with a new light. He wasn't just a pawn to use to further any cause that a planetary government should choose to throw him into. He actually picked the side he wanted to fight on.

"The government of Armenia was a very oppressive government, I remember. And the people were very suppressed. Not very happy. I was glad I could leave. That's why Jeff and I were willing to try to start a new life here."

They had finished eating, so Myrna wanted to show him her house. A woman always wants to show someone her house, Vic thought. It was a fairly roomy house, well kept and clean. It had three bedrooms. And he wondered why she needed three bedrooms. He was starting to figure out that except for her household servants, she lived alone.

After she finished showing him her mansion, they went to the living room. She had Jamie bring them a brandy apiece. "All this could be yours," she said.

Vic didn't expect her to be so blatant nor did he expect her to reveal her motives so suddenly. "But I'd want you to marry me, legally," she continued. "People are rather old fashioned on this planet. They don't have a provision for trial marriages in the social structure, here."

Vic's answer was simple and to the point, "I have a wife back on Ultaria and we're expecting." He didn't mean to be so blunt about it. The words just came out.

Her jaw dropped and the disappointment on her face was obvious. "I thought you were single," she said. "Most spacers are, you know."

"I understand," he explained. "And I also would guess you'd be pretty lonely living here all alone."

"I'm not attracted to the men that were born and raised on this planet," she explained further. "They are just too different from us."

"I can see how that would be," he said.

She paused for a moment and then said, "Is there anyone on your crew that *is* eligible?" she asked quite simply.

"Yes," Vic answered, "But in a military organization you can't just up and abandon your post. That makes you a deserter which is a court martial offense."

"Yes, but the war should be over *someday*, I would hope," she offered in reply. "Or at least it should be possible to complete a period of service obligation?" She worded it as a question instead of a statement.

"It is possible to complete a service obligation. I have a 5 year obligation myself, but I don't know about the war being over. It's lasted as long as I've lived."

"Do you ever have a furlough to visit friends and relatives?" she asked.

"Thirty days a year," he answered.

"Then if I had a man that was in your fleet, he could come calling while he was on leave, and then finally after he completed his service obligation, he could come and marry me and settle down with me,

148

here." One thing Vic liked about her. She'd say just what she meant and explain just what she wanted. Very frank and open. Someone that open had to have a clear conscience, he knew. So that meant she was a good woman. She'd be a good catch for any man that *was* eligible.

"One of my friends is still single. Dan is his name. He's one of the navigators in our crew and a really fine guy. He grew up on the planet Solston, came from the country, in fact. He'd probably like this kind of life."

"Could you introduce him to me?" she asked, hope returning to her voice.

"Sure," he said. "I could have him pay a call on you tomorrow. In the meantime, we need to figure out a way to communicate with our friends in outer space," he decided to tell her his problem since she had apparently finished explaining hers. "The battle damage to our spacecraft destroyed all our radios."

She nodded recognition of the statement he made, then stood up. "Come," she said. He got up and followed her. She walked out of the living room, down the hall to the end, turned left, then turned left again and opened a door. It revealed a stair case. She started up the stairs. He followed. At the top of the stairs was an attic. And there was a table and chair and what looked like an antiquated radio set.

"There are no batteries," she explained. "They wore out years ago. But this is the equipment that Jeff and I used to communicate with friends and relatives back on Armenia in years past. We could send a message to a merchant ship that was within range of this planet and they would relay it to Armenia for us. Jeff had a lot of friends on some of the Armenian merchant ships.

"We have a communications officer in our crew who is an accomplished electrical engineer. He might be able to repair this gear," Vic said.

"But the batteries are completely gone," she explained.

"If he could build a power source, he could get your set to working. And he might be able to salvage some batteries from our wrecked spacecraft for that matter."

"You're welcome to use this equipment if you can get it to work," she explained.

It was getting late enough that Vic decided he could end the evening without offending his hostess. And he was very tired. But the nourishing meal helped to alleviate the fatigue temporarily so he still felt good, though he was ready to go turn in. He made his leave with his hostess and walked out to the barn and found his blankets. He used his back pack for a pillow as he was sure all the other men had done. Within minutes he was asleep.

CHAPTER 38
RESCUE

The following morning when they got up, Vic went over to the pilot in command and filled him in on what he had learned the night before. He explained that the lady that owned the ranch was an extraterrestrial that had emigrated to this planet from Armenia over ten years ago.

"But why did she invite you to the big house for dinner?" he asked.

"To propose to me," was Vic's answer.

"What! She doesn't even know you!" was Hal's reply.

"I know. My jaw dropped about a foot. She said I looked like her late husband. But she has some communication equipment in her attic that she said she'd let us have the loan of if we can repair it. She said that the main problem with it is that the batteries are long gone."

"We can see if they can arrange transportation back to our wrecked spacecraft. Ed can bring back any tools he needs and might find some parts he can salvage," Hal explained.

All the men got ready to walk over to the cook shack for breakfast. The cowboys had already eaten and were gone. Over breakfast, Vic and Hal explained to Ed about what they had in mind. Ed had been a communications engineer before he became a navigator.

After they had finished breakfast, Vic decided it wasn't too early to call on Myrna again. It was nearly 10 o'clock by the sun. So he took both Ed and Dan with him and went and knocked on the door to the big house, again. Jamie opened the door.

"It is too early to call upon Myrna?" Vic asked.

"No," she said, "I'll tell her you are here." He had learned that Jamie did speak Armenian, though she had a foreign accent. She had used her own native language at first since she didn't know what language Vic spoke. But Myrna must have taught her to speak Armenian over the years.

She invited them in to sit down while she went back to tell Myrna they were there. When Myrna walked up, Vic stood and made introductions. "This is our ship's communications engineer, Ed," he explained. Ed was functioning as a communications engineer now, so Vic figured that wasn't too much of a lie. "And this is Dan that I told you about." Dan looked up when he told her that. He didn't know why he had been brought along.

"You can take Ed up and show him the communications set, if you like," Myrna said.

So Vic led Ed back to the stairs and on up to the attic. He left Dan with Myrna. Ed looked at the gear on the table. He lifted a black box and looked at the back of it. He looked around for any additional things in the room that might be included. Then he said, "We need to take a trip out to the wrecked ship. I need my tools and there might be some batteries on the ship that weren't ruined."

So they went downstairs. Jamie met them and escorted them to the dining room again. Myrna and Dan were having a hot drink of some sort. Myrna insisted that Vic and Ed join them. Jamie brought them a cup of the hot beverage each. It was some kind of herbal tea laced with brandy. It was good.

After several sips of the hot drink, Vic explained to Myrna that they needed to go back to their wrecked vessel and salvage some parts from it. She explained that Jimmy, her gardener and handyman, would harness the buckboard and take them wherever they needed to go.

Vic, Ed and Jimmy all managed to fit in the front seat of the buckboard, but just barely. They headed over toward where Vic knew their wrecked space ship to be. It took them a couple of hours to find it. Then Ed got out, found his tool box and started looking for any electronic parts that he thought he might use. Before long he had the back of the buckboard loaded down with his tool box, black boxes, wires and a cooling unit he found on the spacecraft. He thought he could maybe make a turbine to use wind power to run a generator from the cooling unit. And he said he had found several batteries that were still good. They had been brought along as spare batteries and that was probably why they hadn't burned out when the rest of them did. They headed back to the ranch.

When they got back to the ranch house, Jimmy pulled around to the back door this time. He let them in. Jamie had heard them and walked up. Jimmy told her that they had some gear to bring in and take up to the attic. She said, "Fine," and explained that Madam had gone riding with Dan.

Jimmy and Vic helped Ed carry the gear and tools up the stairs. Vic asked him if there was anything else he needed. He asked them to send up Joe, one of the gunners, to help him. He said he was a pretty good technician. He said it would take at least a day to even see if he could get the set to working. He explained that he'd have to build a generator and he'd brought along a cooling unit. He said he thought that maybe he could use the blades to make a windmill. Then the windmill could turn the generator. He was planning to mount it on the roof. This way he could use wind power to operate the generator. So Vic went down and found Joe and had him go up to help Ed.

The rest of the men were sitting in the cook shack playing cards and checkers. Vic figured they needed to occupy their time somehow. If men got too bored they'd get into trouble.

It took Ed and Joe the rest of the day to put together the radio set. They were working on the wind charger and generator when Jamie called them to dinner. Dan found himself sitting at Myrna's table. And he had had a bath and changed into dinner clothes. Myrna's former husband had clothes that fit him fine. Ed and Joe were invited to join them. They politely declined, explaining that their clothes were too dirty from working on the communications gear. So they went out to the cook shack to eat with the hired men.

Ed and Joe couldn't work after dark, of course, because the only light they had was candle light. They decided to wait until morning to test out their wind charger and generator. Then after that they could test out the radio.

So they spent one more night in the barn. The following morning the men had breakfast after the cowboys all left as usual. Then Ed and Joe went and finished up the radio set. Ed notified the pilot in command when they had finished.

Hal walked up the stairs and turned on the radio set. He started trying to reach some space patrol craft that might be in range. After several minutes he finally reached one who in turn relayed their message to the nearest base. It took a few minutes, but then they received a message to the effect that SAR forces would pick them up in about six hours.

Vic talked to Myrna and explained that the New Empire would reimburse her for the food which she had provided to the men if she filed a claim. She flatly explained that they were guests of her ranch. No reimbursement would be necessary! Vic asked for the loan of horses to go to the wrecked spacecraft. That was their rendezvous. She gave her permission and had a horse saddled for herself. She wanted to come along. She decided to bring Jimmy along, too, to bring the horses back.

Six hours later, they were waiting at the wrecked ship when they saw an object come floating down out of the sky. It turned out to be a landing craft. When the men started boarding, they saw another spacecraft coming down getting ready to land. It carried a repair crew and the spare parts they thought would be needed for the wrecked transport ship. They were there to see if they could get the wrecked ship space worthy, the pilot of the rescue craft explained. At any rate they needed to retrieve the cargo and get it on to its destination.

Jimmy seemed to accept the usual happenings without being perturbed especially. So Myrna must have explained to him something about space flight. Vic could imagine the affect it would have had on the cowboys if they all of sudden saw something come out of the sky and land with people getting out of it.

Myrna dismounted and walked with Dan to the landing craft. Then she lifted her head up for a kiss just before he went on board. Then she stood there watching him climb up the ladder. At the top of the ladder he turned and waved and she waved back.

"Remember to send me a message," she called after him as he walked into the entrance hatch.

"Okay," he answered and waved good bye.

CHAPTER 39
BACK ON BASE

When they reached their transport squadron's base, the entire crew had to go through the 30 day quarantine process since they ate food from a foreign planet. It wasn't as big an ordeal this time because they were all quartered together and could play cards and computer games to while away their time. They also were allowed to send messages home, of course. They had been reported as missing in action by then and they naturally wanted to let their loved ones know they were all right.

They started their quarantine with a medical checkup as usual and then had the scheduled checkups during the quarantine to make sure they didn't come down with any contagious disease that might come specifically from that planet.

After the 30 days were up, Vic was assigned to another transport ship and resumed his duties as a transport pilot. They were engaged by enemy forces again several times, but the fighter craft were able to fight them off each time. Finally after two more months their mission of transporting supplies was done and the new base was nearly completed.

Dan sent message disks to Myrna on a regular basis. Communicating with her was a problem at first. The planet had only an archaic paper mail system. And there was no communication link with extraterrestrials. But Myrna had her radio set in the attic. She could send messages to the spaceborne mail ship and they'd put them on disk and forward the disk to Dan. It had audio only, but that was better than nothing. And he found that he could send disks via the mail if he marked it "for transmission to the planet Oltaria" and included Myrna's call sign and frequency. The mail ship would transmit to that call sign on that frequency when they were within range of the planet. He had to pay a premium for this service but he was grateful such a service existed. He planned to take 30 days leave now that their mission was over and get a passenger space liner to let him land on the planet to visit her. He had to get permission from the Task Force Commander to do so, but they had landing craft that they could use to ferry individuals to the surface. He would just have to set a time, date and place for them to pick him up again.

After the work on the new base had been completed, the increased demand for transport pilots had eased somewhat and many of the pilots received orders to new squadrons. Vic received orders to transition school for strike aircraft. That caught him by surprise all over again. He thought he'd go back to flying fighter craft. But these new orders meant he'd be transferred back to the headquarters planet. That's where the school was located, though in a different city from where Red lived. And he was eager to see Red again. He requested 10 days leave and got on a troop transport headed for the home planet. After the 10 days leave was up there would still be time to report to strike spacecraft school. Red would be four months pregnant by now.

When Vic landed on Ultaria at the space port and debarked from the space craft, he saw Red in the crowd at the off loading ramp. She was wearing maternity clothes this time. But she was barely showing. He walked up to her and reached down to kiss her and she grabbed him and gave him a bear hug.

"Careful, don't squeeze little tyke," he cautioned.

"It won't hurt anything. It's going to be a boy, you know."

Pregnant women were so reckless he thought, but he didn't want to make an issue of it. He was just so glad to see her. And she thought it was going to be a boy. He hadn't told her otherwise. He figured it wouldn't hurt to keep it a secret for now.

She had brought his red flying saucer. And she wanted him to drive. So he loaded his luggage in the luggage compartment and then held the door while she climbed into the passenger seat. He then secured the door and he went around to the driver's seat and climbed in.

"Our address is about to be changed," she told him.

"It is?"

"Yes, we have a house now. Daddy gave us a house as a wedding present. It just wasn't ready for us to move into before you left."

"Don't move in, yet. I have orders to start strike spacecraft training. And it's at Crafton which is on the other side of the continent."

"Oh?" she didn't know.

"I didn't know until a week ago, myself," he explained.

So Vic flew to her apartment. He sat down his little ship on the roof of her apartment complex as gently as he could and they got out. He took his luggage down the steps and to her apartment. He sat them inside. She followed him. He wouldn't let her carry anything. After setting his luggage down, Vic turned her side ways and then hugged her again, reaching down to give her a long kiss. She tolerated his fatherly protectiveness. She knew it was a good quality in a man.

He explained how he had 10 days leave before reporting to his new duty station. And she told him he should pay a call on the Admiral within a few days. He still didn't feel completely comfortable in the presence of admirals while she was completely comfortable with people no matter how high in rank whether it was social or military. But he knew he should see his father-in-law every once in a while.

Vic and Red decided to visit the Admiral two days hence. That would give them time to get packed and ready to move. They decided to go ahead and pack and move and then take the rest of their vacation time in the vicinity of Crafton. It would be new country they hadn't seen before.

Chapter 40
Strike Pilot

So Vic started his training, ground school first, as usual, then simulators and then started logging time in the spacecraft itself. He found himself doing practice take offs and landings in the S10910M, a medium sized strike spacecraft. Its nickname was Striker 2. The small version of the strike spacecraft was Striker 1 and the heavy version was called Striker 3. The Striker 2 carried a crew of two: pilot and bombardier/navigator. And he found he landed it on its belly in a fashion similar to how the transports landed rather than on its tail. It made loading ordnance easier. And take offs and landings were easier, too. But then, even the fighter craft had to land on their belly when bringing them aboard a spacecraft carrier as far as that goes. The increased gravity force made it necessary for a fighter craft to land on its tail when on a planet surface. But it could land on its belly with the very light gravity of a space ship. Striker 2 had two laser torpedo guns in the nose and two bomb racks on each side that could handle either laser bombs or high explosives. It also had a tail laser gun to shoot at anyone that attacked from behind. The bombardier/navigator didn't come along on the initial training flights. He wouldn't be needed until the pilot started training on simulated strikes.

After the new pilots mastered the art of takeoff and landing, they did their instrument training. Then formation flying was next. This was especially critical because they'd normally attack in formation. After they'd mastered formation flying they worked on formation flying in outer space. Then after that they focused their attention on low level flying. For low level flying they would fly to a planet that had an uninhabited area and just skim the planet's surface. And he found out the reason the particular planet for their training had been chosen. There was a desert that had both sandy and rocky areas. And there was lots of ocean. This way they could practice low level flying over both land and water. The trick to flying low over water was to just be high enough above the water not to create any spray.

After flying all day, he'd return home to Red. She'd either prepare food or just have prepared food delivered to their quarters. They found the married couples quarters on the base adequate for their needs. They knew they'd be there only a few months, anyway.

* * *

Vic took off in his strike spacecraft and headed for the nearby mountains. It was his first solo flight in this type of spacecraft. You had to fly several solo flights and do your own navigating as part of your training so this time his navigator/bombardier wasn't on board.

When Vic reached the mountains his altitude was 500 feet above the terrain. He headed for a saddle between two mountains. The armament pods had been removed from his spacecraft. So his strike spacecraft had kind of the shape of a saucer only it had a slight point to the nose and a slight recession on the tail. With no ordnance attached to it there was very little drag to slow his speed. He zoomed through the saddle between the two mountains at about 50 feet above the ground. There was a valley beyond so he dipped his nose to get lower. He maintained 100 feet above the terrain until he approached the mountains on the other side. Then he raised his nose and headed for another saddle on the other side.

This kind of flying is fun, thought Vic. The mountains were for the most part uninhabited. Vic had heard that a few mountain people lived there, but no cities or towns. When Vic zoomed through the next saddle, he had a hundred miles or so of desert ahead of him. The terrain was flat as a pancake. He got down as low as he could to avoid fogging up sand. He found that was about 100 feet. At 50 feet he could see a dust storm stirring up in his wake in his rear view mirrors. He moved the throttle forward to hypersonic speed. At the end of the desert was ocean. He adjusted his altitude just barely above the altitude in which spray kicked up behind him. He discovered this was about 75 feet or so. The water below him was zooming by really fast. He really got a thrill from the sensation of traveling this fast this close to the ocean.

It was only minutes before he came to a volcanic island chain. He slowed his speed to subsonic as he approached. He maneuvered his ship in between two volcanic mountains. He avoided a village on the left side of one of the volcanoes. And he couldn't imagine why anyone would build a village near a volcanic mountain. He had to make a series of steep turns to avoid each mountain that he came to. He was threading in and around them like as if running a maze. At the other end he knew there would be several thousand miles of ocean again. So he pulled his nose up, increased speed and headed for outer space. Within a few minutes he was floating free of the planet's atmosphere.

He orbited the planet for half a revolution, and then started a descent to enter above a mountainous area on the opposite side of the planet from where he started. The planet seemed to come up slowly at first. It just gradually got larger, barely noticeable. But as he got closer it started coming up faster. He reduced his speed and applied his antigravity braking device. He was subsonic by the time he leveled off a thousand feet or so above the mountain tops.

Then he dipped down below the mountain tops and resumed his low level maneuvering, flying around mountains, through saddles and in some cases, just skimming over the top of a mountain peak.

After he had completed all the exercises in low level flying that he was scheduled for he zoomed up toward the heavens again. He put his spacecraft up into outer space and orbited to a position just above home base. He re-entered the atmosphere brought her in for a landing. My, but that flight was fun. And Ted, his navigator/bombardeir, missed out on it.

CHAPTER 41
DINOSAURS

Vic and Ted took off. They went into outer space and headed for another planet. They were on a training flight to simulate an actual strike. The planet was an uninhabited planet that was known to be in the stage in which they still had dinosaurs, saber tooth tigers and other such animals that lived in that era.

They left the planet's atmosphere and Ted put the coordinates of their destination planet into the navigational computer. Vic liked having Ted along. While he had logged many hours of solo flight he had to admit that flying was more fun when you had company.

It took them a couple of hours before they started approaching their destination planet. Vic eased the ship into orbit and waited until Ted gave him the word that it was time to ease on down to the planet's atmosphere.

After they were inside the atmosphere, Vic went into a steep dive to get down near the terrain as soon as possible. He headed for a mountainous area. He knew he still needed more low level training amongst mountains. He flew over a mountain peak at about 50 feet of altitude above the terrain and then eased on down into a canyon dotted with tall trees. He pulled the throttle back and slowed down to the minimum flying speed. Then he found a valley and eased on down to about 20 feet above the ground. He flew the length of valley and pulled the nose up just in time to fly over some tree tops. He missed the tree tops by a good 10 feet. Ted sucked in his breath. He wasn't accustomed to flying *this* low over trees. But Vic knew he needed the training at flying this low. They were too low to be detected by any kind of detection gear. Of course this planet was uninhabited except for the primitive animals that populated the planet. But this was how low they would need to fly on an actual mission in some cases.

Vic then pulled up the nose of the spacecraft to fly through a saddle between two mountains. Then after he passed the saddle he eased the nose down again. They were now past the mountains and headed toward a plain that was still dotted with a few trees and had a few rocky places. Vic was still flying at his minimum flying speed. He went down to 20 feet above the terrain again. Then he saw a herd of dinosaurs. The dinosaurs looked up to see the slow flying machine headed toward them and they spooked, scattering in all different directions. They knocked down trees and boulders wherever they went. Vic and Ted couldn't help but laugh at the havoc they caused as they pulled up just enough to avoid hitting any of the stampeding dinosaurs. This meant the dinosaurs must have been more than 20 feet tall. They were huge.

* * *

On their next mission they had a training exercise scheduled for the same planet but this time a flight of four spacecraft participated in the mission. Vic led the flight. They now did their maneuvering down low amongst the mountains and in the canyons and valleys with a flight of four spacecraft maintaining formation. And when they got to the plains, Vic deliberately went looking for the herd of dinosaurs. He saw them in the distance, just little tiny specks. Vic gave the signal over the radio to the other pilots that he was going to go supersonic. So four spacecraft flew low over the dinosaur herd and created four simultaneous sonic booms. He saw the blur as their spacecraft passed by just over their heads. The dinosaurs really did go nuts this time. There was probably an area 100 yards wide completely cleared of trees and boulders. Vic called the flight over the radio and told them he was going subsonic now. He circled around and flew over the spot slowly. You could still see the stampeding dinosaurs in several different directions and uprooted trees lying everywhere. Vic couldn't help but laugh and he knew the other pilots were doing likewise.

"You're cruel," Simon, one of the pilots said over the radio.

"Yeah, but they needed exercise," Vic returned.

Then Vic pulled up and headed the flight back into the outer space. Their entertainment over, he decided it was time to conclude the training exercise and head back for home.

* * *

After the pilots mastered the basics of flying their spacecraft they started making their simulated strikes, though Vic and several of the pilots had already flown several. There was an area out in the desert that was very rocky. And this area was about 5 miles or so in diameter. So they used that as a simulated enemy base. Ted navigated the spacecraft to and from the target area. Once over the target area, Ted handled firing the laser torpedoes and dropping the laser bombs. This way Vic could concentrate his time on jinking to avoid being hit by ground fire or fighter craft. And Vic had a nose laser and a firing button on his control stick so he could fire at any threats directly in front of them himself if need be.

Toward the end of Vic's training in the new spacecraft, a series of lectures were scheduled to educate them in tactics and strategy. He learned the reason why they were beefing up the strike forces of the fleet. The New Empire was growing while the Old Empire continued to shrink. Of course, Vic understood the reason for that. That's where he came from himself. But he learned that an active campaign was continually in force to encourage as many trained spacers and soldiers to defect to the New Empire as was possible. This created the problem of making sure that spies couldn't infiltrate their ranks. But the effective screening measures developed by the Admiral had made it possible to detect them very reliably. If they were determined to be a plant, they were court martialed and shot. But the ones that actually wanted to fight for the right to pursue a life of personal freedom for the individual were welcomed with open arms and assimilated into the New Empire forces with enthusiasm.

New strategic bases had been planned and were being built on planets not held by either the Old or New Empire and they had been fighting strictly a defensive war until they could get these bases established.

But, of course, the admirals in the Old Empire had not been idle. They found out that the New Empire was expanding and so had stepped up their attacks on the New Empire shipping since they knew that new bases were being built to expand their area of control.

Predations from the Old Empire against New Empire shipping

had reached the point that mere defense was no longer a viable strategy. So a campaign to attack Old Empire bases had been in the planning stages, but was now ready to begin. They all got orders to various squadrons to deploy aboard a spacecraft carrier and launch their campaign.

This meant Vic had to part with Red again. She got ready to move back to Seaside to their new house. She figured at least she could be near her father while Vic was gone.

He loaded up his gear into the red saucer and she flew him to the space port.

CHAPTER 42
VIC JOINS THE SPACECRAFT CARRIER

Vic felt nervous when he and Ted went out to man the spacecraft. It was their day to fly up and join the spacecraft carrier. He just felt like there was a knot in his gut. He always felt nervous just before a flight but it was more so today than usual. They went through their checklists and lifted off. They joined up in formation with a flight of four other newly graduated strike pilots. They flew with the flight on up into outer space.

When they arrived at the carrier, they each had to bring their ship into the recovery bay. For each of them it was the first time for that type of spacecraft. When it came Vic's turn he brought her in and he could tell he was a little too fast. He felt the tenseness even more than usual and his left arm and shoulder started to hurt. He had landed fighter craft on spacecraft carriers many times, but this was his first time to bring a strike craft on board. And he hadn't landed on a spacecraft carrier in six months.

"Slow her down," he heard the flight control officer call over the radio. He pulled the throttle back. The landing bay loomed larger.

"You're too slow, now, get some more power on," was the next call over the radio. He adjusted the power. He finally got her through the landing bay door and brought her to a hover four feet off the flight deck. A taxi director gave him the signals to park his spacecraft and he went through his secure checklist. He and Ted climbed out. Then they went to the squadron commander's office to report in.

They found Commander Jacks in his office. Ted remained outside while Vic went through the door and saluted.

"Ensign Mabry reporting for duty, sir," he said.

"At ease," he said, "And you have your rank wrong," he added. "Your promotion to Half Lieutenant just arrived," he said with a smile.

Half Lieutenant Mabry smiled, too. He didn't expect a promotion just yet. After a brief conversation in keeping with protocol he was dismissed and an orderly was sent with him to show him to his quarters. Ted entered the commander's office just as he left.

The following morning they had a briefing in the ready room. He found that the ship was en route to their operating area and that they would be flying patrols while en route.

But first, they had to have some more practice taking off and landing on the spacecraft carrier itself. Vic checked the flight schedule and found out he was scheduled to fly at 1400 hours. He put on his flight suit and went to man up. He still felt nervous. A little jittery. It wasn't necessary for Ted to come along for this flight since he wouldn't go far from the spacecraft carrier.

He got the drives started and on the signal from the taxi director he lifted off and headed for the landing bay door. He launched into the black goo. They had one bay door open for launching and another for recoveries. But since they had several squadrons practicing take-offs and landings they had three sets of doors open. He had to maintain the proper interval on the spacecraft ahead of him. It was tedious. His first landing was a little rough. He didn't touch down but brought her in and held it in a hover four feet off the deck per procedure until the flight director signaled him to take off again. The landing bay doors were open on both sides of the landing deck so all he did was just get in motion again and head out the opposite door. The second landing was smoother.

On his 3rd landing approach Vic saw the spacecraft coming in to land on the landing bay to his right fly right into the side of the landing bay door. It cart wheeled and crashed inside the landing bay.

"All spacecraft, stop your approach," Vic heard the flight control officer's voice over the radio. Vic pulled his machine to a quick stop. "Hover away from the carrier until the landing deck is cleared."

So Vic put his ship in a hover and had to wait until the wreckage was cleared in the landing bay. It took about fifteen minutes. Vic wondered if the pilot was injured or not. But then flight operations were resumed and Vic got his remaining practice recoveries.

After 5 landings they were considered fully spacecraft carrier qualified. Then they had their scheduled patrol flights.

So Vic was back to flying daily. The patrols were boring, as usual, but his daily routine was different.

And he found the Communications office so he could send Red message disks again. It was refreshing to get to see her face again when he received one of her disks.

CHAPTER 43
LEAVING

Jules made Nina some moccasins. She watched closely because she wanted to learn how to do it. He explained to her that boots were better for wearing on the trail unless you needed to move quietly. And her boots were still okay. But moccasins would help keep her feet warm at night while she was sleeping. After he finished the first moccasin she asked him if she could make the other one. So he handed her the tools and a piece of leather and watched her work.

The next morning Jules explained that he had to leave for a few hours. In fact, he might be gone all day. And he cautioned her not to leave the cave for any reason while he was gone. He felt confident by now that she'd follow his instructions. She wasn't near the burden that he thought she would be but he didn't dare take her with him, of course.

He had a pair of snow shoes near the entrance of the cave and put them on over his moccasins before he left. He was wearing his winter moccasins. They came halfway up his calf and had fur on the inside so they were a little bigger than his summer moccasins. After he left Nina decided she needed something to occupy herself while he was gone. So she rummaged through his box of leather working gear. She found some old moccasins that she could use for a pattern for making new ones. They had fur on the inside so they were for winter. She found some kind of animal skin that had fur on one side and decided she'd try to make him a new pair since the ones he was wearing looked like they were nearly worn out.

Jules trudged through the snow. It took several hours to get near his destination. It was about 10 miles or so and he couldn't make more than about 3 miles per hour walking through snow on his snow shoes.

He stuck to a trail frequently used by mountain men until he reached a point that was heading up hill and he rounded a bend. Then he left the trail and started walking through the brush. At this point he took a pine branch and dragged it behind him to cover up his tracks. You could still see the snow had been disturbed if you looked up close but there were no tracks showing from the main trail. He worked his way in and around brush up to a place near the top of a mountain. As he grew closer to his destination he was careful to disguise his tracks more carefully. He saw what looked like the front of a cabin built against a cliff face. But if it was a cabin it was really small. Not big enough for more than a bunk and a stove. He stopped at a tree and reached up to a bell that was tied to a lower limb. He rang the bell and then waited.

Very shortly a man appeared. Jules said, "Wood."

The man said, "Fire."

Jules was holding his crossbow at the ready with a bolt ready to fire. He would have shot him if he hadn't given the correct counter password. But then the man was holding a rifle. He would have shot Jules if he hadn't given the correct password.

Jules started walking toward the cabin. The man fell in step beside him. The man knocked on the door twice, paused, then twice more.

"Enter," he heard a voice say from inside.

The man opened the door and stepped aside while Jules entered, closing the door behind him.

There was a man sitting beside a fire and a woman sitting in a kneeling position nursing a baby. She made no attempt to cover her exposed breast. Jules knew that he had a flue built just above the fire to direct the smoke out to the top of the cliff above where it would disburse among the branches of trees. And the room was much larger that you would expect. The structure had been dug into a cave that extended into the cliff face.

"Hello Abe," Jules said.

"Hello Jules," Abe returned. He had a gray beard about four inches long and you could tell he was well built though he was sitting down. He was puffing a pipe.

"Come up to the fire and sit," Abe said. Jules complied.

"And what is the reason for your trip?" Abe asked.

"I've come to tell you that I accept the mission."

"Hmmm," and he paused for a minute. "There must be a reason for your change of mind."

"There is." And he told him about Nina and how his main cave was now compromised.

The woman nursing the baby put the little one over her shoulder and patted its back to make it burp. It started crying when its meal was interrupted. You could barely hear it when it burped. The woman didn't bother to cover her breast until she took the baby from her shoulder and got her other breast out and allowed the little one to resume its meal.

"We can get her on the next smuggler ship going out," Abe then said.

"But you told me that the one she was scheduled on was shot down with all hands lost. The captain was the one that had her money. Captains will sometimes cooperate and return the money to another captain if someone has to change a flight. But that captain is dead. She has no money."

"So you plan to take her with you. If she was your woman her passage would be free."

"Yes."

"I hate to lose you but as I told you before you are better qualified than anyone else I've got for this mission."

* * *

Nina completed the moccasins and had started making a new deerskin jacket for Jules by the time she saw light suddenly shine in the door. She sucked in her breath in panic at first when she saw the patch of brush removed from the door of the cave. Then she relaxed when she saw Jules' face. He stooped down to enter the cave and was dragging a deer behind him. He had a tripod of branches just inside the cave where he hung the deer, head up. Then he removed his snowshoes.

There was a stack of wood on the opposite wall. Jules carried a armful of wood to the fireplace and started making a fire. When Nina saw what he was doing she came to help him. Jules reached inside the body cavity of the deer and brought out the liver. He placed it on a rock and started slicing off pieces. Nina found a skillet and greased it and started frying it.

So they could finally have a fire, she thought. That must mean that Jules had determined that no Imperial forces were nearby. Jules reached into his backpack and took out some fresh potatoes and onions. He found a tea pot in one of the boxes and rummaged some more to find some store bought tea! So they had a better meal than Nina could remember having in a long time.

It wasn't until then that Nina remembered the moccasins she had made for Jules. She showed them to him. He removed the moccasins he was wearing and tried them on. They fit perfectly. He didn't say anything but she could tell by the look on his face that he was pleased. Then he saw the coat she had been working on. He reached over and squeezed her hand.

That afternoon Jules skinned out the deer. He rigged a tripod near the fire to hang it on. After he skinned it he salted the hide, folded it up and laid it against the wall to drain. Then they sat down and had another cup of tea and relaxed for awhile.

When it came near time for dinner, Jules took his belt knife and started cutting steaks from the back of the deer. Nina started some potatoes and onions to boil and Jules took a grid and propped it over the fire with stones and started the steaks to broiling. When the food was done, Jules went to one of the boxes and pulled out a bottle of wine. They had gourmet meal! Nina thought that Jules lived really well when he was in his own cave. Things he had bought from the black market, obviously.

After another two weeks, Jules escorted Nina to her new group of refugees and disappeared in the forest. She saw the spacecraft land and they made ready to board the ship. She was trying to fight back the tears. She knew she'd never see Jules again. And she didn't like the way the men among the passengers looked at her. She felt scared. There were a few women in the crowd but most of them were just as rangy looking as the men. She was totally oblivious to the fact that she looked irresistible in her tight fitting leather pants. And she had formed the habit of wearing her long hair down her back since she found out that Jules liked it that way. Tears were streaming down her face when she boarded the craft and found a vacant seat. But there was nothing else she knew to do.

Then to her surprise, just before the spacer closed the hatch she saw Jules climb in. He found a seat and strapped in just before they took off. He sat in a seat just in front of the entrance hatch one row ahead of her. If she had known he was going to come along she would have saved him a seat next to her!

CHAPTER 44
ARMY TROOPS

Three troop transports were in orbit around the planet Astro. A soldier's life is mainly hurry and wait and it seems like he spends more time waiting than hurrying. They were cramped in the tight quarters. A full regiment on each ship. They were waiting for word to land forces on the planet.

In addition to the three troop transports were three cargo ships loaded with flying tanks and gravity trucks loaded with the necessary soldiers to man them. The intention to take and occupy the planet Astro was now obvious. So it would be necessary to land troops on every continent. But the advanced force would be these three regiments with their tanks and trucks. They would make sure they secured each continent and established the necessary supply lines to maintain the troops in the field.

So they played cards and told jokes and talked about women they'd seen on their last leave. Computer games weren't feasible due to the mass of men cramped into their tight spaces. And besides, they didn't have any computers. A soldier's life is mostly boring. If you weren't bored, you were terrified, so boredom was probably the better of the two. Until you've been bored too long. Then you reached the point you'll do anything to alleviate the boredom.

The men on the ships didn't lack much being to that point. They were ready for some action. Anything to get off the cramped confines of the space ship.

But even worse was the suspense. They were waiting for orders but they didn't know how long they'd have to wait. They had to just continue their orbit until they finally received word to land troops and equipment on the planet's surface. They had rations three times a day but there weren't enough bunks for all the men. Some of them just rolled up in their blankets in the passageways. At least they were warm and dry. Those were two things that a soldier couldn't always count on.

For now they were just boring holes in space. On and on and on. Stark boredom and cramped confines. For anything at all to happen would be better than to have nothing happen.

There was another feeling that the men could feel once the battle had been joined. That was anger. To see their buddies fall to enemy fire could instill into them both hate and anger. And this resulted in a massive relief for their pent up emotions. That wasn't something they'd think about or could look forward to. They didn't look that far ahead. They now just felt a combination of boredom and anxiety. They each had an unpleasant feeling in their belly. But they still had no choice but to just endure. And wish something would happen.

CHAPTER 45
GUERILLA TROOPS EN ROUTE TO TARGET

The ship was packed with men and women. All of them wore shabby clothes, even the ship's crew. The Fleet didn't mix men and women in the same regiments due to the problems in discipline that resulted. They didn't worry about it with guerilla troops. They dealt with problems of discipline by simply shooting the offender. While there were men inclined to rape and ravage some of the women, two of them were already dead, now. They had been shot for trying to achieve their amorous purposes even before they had left the planet Armenia. So there were no more disciplinary problems, at least thus far.

The Captain was on the bridge monitoring the view screen. They were headed for the planet Astro. The men and women in the hold were all recruits from the defectors to the New Empire. All were defectors with three exceptions. Criminals and political prisoners had been freed from a prison on the planet Armenia. But mostly criminals. And with a reason. Burglars and assassins. That was one exception. They did not have to pay a fee to be smuggled off the planet. Their fee was paid for by the New Empire. They had a specific mission.

And three of them were plants. That was another exception. Spies that had infiltrated their way into the group. Captain Keg had that bit of intelligence from a reliable source. But he had a standard procedure for dealing with them.

The third exception was Jules and Nina. Jules' mission was the extraction of the burglars and assassins into the mountains after they had completed their mission. Nina was along just because Jules insisted on bringing her along.

For now the captain was mainly interested in making sure there were no Imperial ships in the area. His ship had a nose laser gun and a tail gun but it still would be no match for Imperial fighter craft if they encountered them so it was imperative that he remain undetected.

This ship was a smugglers' ship and relied on choosing a path in which Imperial ships did not travel.

When he was over half the distance to his destination, he nodded to his first mate. First Officer Heimer Kimmel nodded in turn and went through the after hatch to the hold where the passengers were huddled in their crowded spaces. Two spacers where standing watch over the passengers. He pulled the manifest out of his hip pocket and called the names of three of the passengers. They pulled themselves up out of their crowded positions and came forward. He explained that the Captain wanted to see them.

When they arrived at the bridge, the Captain explained that they had been chosen to serve as officers on this mission when they arrived on Astro. That the guerillas would be divided into three groups and each of them would lead one of the groups. He explained that he needed to brief them on their mission and that the maps they needed had not been brought in from the air lock, yet. The First Officer opened the air lock door to let them go retrieve the three boxes of maps.

As soon as the third spy had stepped through the hatch into the airlock, the First Officer immediately closed the hatch and locked it down. Then he moved the lever which opened the outer hatch. The vacuum from outer space, of course, sucked all three men out the outer hatch into space. Their blood evaporated immediately and they were dead before they had a chance to freeze to death from the intense cold. Outer space is at absolute zero. So they would have frozen to death if their eyes had not popped out of their heads first and their ear drums burst from the immediate change to a total vacuum.

So that job was done. Now they only needed to arrive at their destination, get the ship into the atmosphere of the planet Astro and get them in position to make their jump.

Nina looked over at Jules. He was sitting four seats over and one row ahead of her. She could see the profile of his face but couldn't read anything from his facial expression. She never could. And she couldn't discern anything about his feelings from his manner. He just sat there with a deadpan expression on his face and seemed completely comfortable just being idle and doing nothing. But she could sense his feelings anyway. And she knew that anxiety was totally foreign to his nature. But she could sense that he was full of anticipation. It was like as if he was eager to reach their destination.

But she couldn't understand why she was aboard. She sensed the tension in the atmosphere and had concluded that this space ship wasn't just full of refugees. There was something else going on here though she didn't know what.

But she was glad that Jules hadn't stayed behind. The idea of never seeing him again had filled her with grief. She was nervous and uneasy but at least there was some chance that she'd get to spend time with Jules again though that was something she didn't really know for sure.

For now she was glad that they had left Armenia. She wished she knew where they were going though she dared not ask.

CHAPTER 46
MAJOR STRIKE

Vic was sitting in the ready room. The briefing for a major air strike was in progress. Commander Jacks was giving them their briefing.

"You will enter the atmosphere on the planet on the side opposite to the location of the enemy base. You'll approach the base from the ocean. There'd be no anti-spacecraft fire there. And stay low, barely high enough not to churn up spray from the water. Since we'll be flying at 2,000 miles per hour this will be at about 500 feet.

"When you reach land you'll go straight across a desert. The desert is 2000 miles long, and then you'll go across a mountain range. And stay low while crossing the desert, too. Barely high enough not to churn up dust from the desert surface. And when you cross the mountains stay to the northern extreme of the mountain range. Anti-spacecraft fire will be lighter there."

"Okay. Time to go man up. Good luck."

They left the ready room and made their way to the launching bay. Vic and Ted climbed into their strike craft and started their checklists. When it came their turn, the taxi director directed them into position to launch. They left the launching bay and formed up. Then started their flight to the enemy planet. They were headed for the planet, Astro. The flight leader's navigator, of course, was responsible for making sure they entered the planet's atmosphere at the right location. Ted would do his calculations on his computer, too, for double checking purposes. But they'd remain in formation the whole time.

When they entered the planet's atmosphere they kept descending, Vic saw nothing but deep blue water as far as the eye could see. They changed to a loose trail formation to enable more maneuverability and continued their descent until Vic's altimeter showed 500 feet. They maintained 500 feet for 10,000 miles per their briefing. It took them 5 hours to finally site land. Then nothing but sand. Big sand dunes, no vegetation whatsoever. 2,000 miles of desert. They maintained their altitude as low as they could and still not stir up the sand on the surface. Crossing the desert took an hour. It was night time by the time they reached the mountains. This would make flying over the mountains more tedious but the enemy had to depend on instruments only to detect them this way.

The squadron commander led them across the northern edge of the mountains, as he had briefed them. After they crossed the mountains, he gave one command, "Arm." Then the Commander led them in on their first bombing run. Vic was still the leader of his division of 4 spacecraft. They encountered no enemy fire while crossing the mountains. They crossed the mountains at the northern end as briefed. Then made a wide turn to head south over the enemy base.

When they neared the base, the lead aircraft immediately started dropping bombs on their selected targets. The barracks were hit first, then the officer's quarters. The headquarters building then got a pounding. When Vic's flight got over the base they started dropping bombs on any spacecraft that they saw parked outside. They used high explosive bombs this time because they wanted to destroy the spacecraft but not obliterate the base completely. They'd have a use for it themselves after it was captured.

Then the anti-spacecraft fire finally started up. They apparently had some benefit from the element of surprise. At the end of their bombing run, Vic turned right, flew a race track pattern and then started another bombing run. Vic jinked his spacecraft very skillfully and managed to dodge ground fire successfully for another run. There were at least 100 ships engaged in the attack in all, counting fighter craft. When Vic maneuvered his flight around for another bombing run he found himself at the tail end of a massive strike force.

After a third run, Vic's bombs were gone. He still had laser torpedoes and his laser guns to defend himself with. But the briefing called for three bombing runs. So he led his flight straight up to leave the planet's atmosphere as briefed. A massive barrage of ground fire erupted from the mountain peaks as soon as they got above 1,000 feet or so. The gun emplacements on the peaks of the mountains were there to prevent any enemy forces from crossing the mountains. The anti-space gun couldn't fire while they were making their bombing runs because as low as they were flying, they'd be hitting their own base. Now they were up high enough that they could shoot at them.

Vic saw ships falling from the sky in flames on both sides on pull out from all three bombing runs but it was even worse now. He jinked like crazy but felt his ship lurch with a deafening explosion. He kept flying. He checked all his instruments. His defensive shield had been damaged. One more hit in that same place and it would be all over.

He was already climbing at maximum speed, though the maneuvering he was doing to avoid being hit again slowed his climb. In a few minutes he was finally out of range of the ground artillery.

Then he saw enemy fighter craft aloft. Their own fighter screen had already engaged them but the enemy fighters were attacking the strike aircraft whenever they got a chance. Vic saw an enemy fighter head for him on his scope. He immediately pulled the nose up to meet the assault and fired his lasers as soon as the enemy fighter was in range. It disappeared off his scope. Okay, that was one more.

Vic managed to shoot down two more enemy fighters before he was finally clear of the melee. Then he checked with his flight to see how they fared. Only one answered. Two apparently had been shot down.

Vic had the one remaining spacecraft in his flight fly close to him and visually inspect his spacecraft outside to see if he could better appraise the damage. Silva was his name. Silva told him his hull was damaged, but that he should be able to land her okay.

Vic brought his spacecraft back and landed her on the mother ship. Then he said, "Whew!", before he unstrapped and climbed out.

At the debriefing he learned that 26 spacecraft had been shot down in all during the raid. SAR spacecraft were being launched to look for any survivors.

* * *

The next day another strike was scheduled. Vic went to the wardroom to grab breakfast. And Vic wondered about yesterday. Why didn't the "power" warn him of the enemy ground fire before it hit him. His "power" had been very reliable before. But then it didn't prevent him from crashing two spacecraft and bringing back a third with considerable battle damage. So apparently it doesn't help enough if you're battered with the kind of massive fire that they caught from the mountain peaks yesterday.

A skilled tactical commander knows not to do the same thing twice. Not in succession, at least. So this day they approached the enemy base from the west, over the water. They flew over the bay just skimming the waves and popped up just before they reached the city and made their turn to the right. They had to get high enough to clear the sky scrapers. The commercial district of the city was right on the water. The enemy fleet base was just a little to the southeast of the city. The mountains were to the left of the base.

They armed switches on the command of the strike leader and started their bombing runs. The fighter spacecraft preceded them and came in above them to engage any enemy fighter craft that managed to get airborne. Vic's targets were the launch pads this time but anytime he saw an enemy spacecraft he took the time to shoot it down with his nose laser, as always.

Five bombing runs this time. They really pounded the enemy base. They finally succeeded in the destruction of the landing pads.

CHAPTER 47
GUERILLA TROOPS JUMP

When the smuggler ship arrived in orbit around the planet, the first mate went back to the hold and told the guerilla troops it was time to don their parachutes. They had no back pack rocket equipment and had to use old fashioned parachutes made of fabric. The ship moved out of orbit and headed for the enemy base. The time was midnight.

There was an aisle down the middle of the ship with the rows of seats on both sides. Jules brought Nina her parachute and told her to stand up. She looked up and he could see the fear on her face in the dim light. He helped her put it on. He placed her hand on the D-ring and explained that when they jumped she would count to ten and then pull out the ring and pull down hard. She said, "I hope I can remember," with a tremor to her voice.

"You will jump just before I do," he explained.

When they were below 10,000 feet, the officers went back and told the guerillas it was time to get ready to jump. At 0200 the mate opened the airlock doors and told the men and women to jump. It was the first time for any of them. They had been briefed on how to control their descent by pulling on the risers. The men and women jumped in pairs, one burglar and one assassin to each pair. They were to land on top of the roofs of the senior officers' quarters.

When all of the guerillas had jumped except Jules and Nina and one other woman, the first mate went back to tell her it was time for her to jump, too. She refused to jump. Her name was Maria. So the mate directed two spacers to take her by each arm and they drug her to the airlock door. They threw her into the inner airlock bodily. Then the spacers went into the inner airlock compartment and one of the spacers placed her hand on the D ring for the rip cord and told her to hold her hand on it and pull on it just after she got clear of the spacecraft. Then the two spacers grabbed her and threw her out the outer lock door, too.

She was in a state of panic at the time she left the ship. But she remembered to pull her rip cord. So her chute opened okay. She saw flashlights flashing on momentarily and then off all around her as she floated down. It was a dark night and that was the only way they could tell if they were floating toward their targets.

Then it was time for Nina to jump. She closed her eyes and took a dive out of the main entrance hatch. Jules followed her. It was pitch dark. Jules shined his flashlight on Nina. She was tugging on her rip cord. She couldn't get it loose. Then she put her hands over her eyes and he could hear her screaming.

He placed his hands in front of him and straightened his body with his hands pointed straight toward her to cut down drag and increase his rate of fall. When he reached her he fastened one hand to her chest strap and pulled her D-ring with the other hand. Her chute opened with a snap and he felt the heavy jerk against his left hand. He held on while he pulled his own D-ring. When his own chute opened he released her chest strap and pushed away from her. He floated out so there was about 30 or 40 feet of space between them.

"Are you okay?" he called.

"I think so," was the feeble answer he heard.

"Pull on your right riser with both hands," he told her. When she did so he did the same. He wanted them to land at the eastern outskirts of town. He used his flashlight to pick out the tops of the sky scrapers so he could get them headed in the direction he wanted them to go.

When Maria's chute opened she seemed to come back to life and remembered to pull on her risers to guide her descent to the tops of one of the buildings as briefed. She landed on the roof. Olney was already on the roof. Once she landed and discarded her parachute, the panic she felt was gone. She drew her dagger and moved in behind Olney. He was the lock picker that would open the door for her.

Olney picked the lock to the roof access door and she went in. She went down the stairs, found the bedroom of the base commander. Olney had followed her and moved ahead of her as she stepped aside. Then he picked that lock for her as well. All the guards were on the ground. They had not anticipated an attack from the roof.

Maria slipped inside to the base commander's bed and brought her dagger down hard into the sleeping form. She stabbed him in the chest four or five times. Then she wiped her dagger on the bed sheets and turned around to follow Olney to their next target. She managed to kill four senior officers before the building was secure. There were several other teams that landed on this same building.

So with all the enemy officers in the building dead, they worked their way to the ground floor. Their mission was accomplished. Now extraction was their next priority.

Of fifty-three guerillas that jumped, six were killed when they landed and another eight either had broken bones or badly sprained ankles. That left thirty-nine to do the job. Now their job was to get away from the base before the next air raid from the New Empire started. Their instructions were to head for the mountains to the east of the base.

Hans was one of the defectors. He had had some medical training. He had five other defectors that has been assigned to help him. His job was to rescue the wounded, if possible. So his team collected the eight injured guerillas. They fashioned a stretcher by stretching a piece of parachute silk across two rifles. They had to make two stretchers. One of the wounded had a broken leg and another had a badly sprained ankle.

The moon had risen by then so they had some light to make their way but they also had to avoid being seen by any guards. Thus it was still tedious but the worst part of their mission was past. They knew all along that extraction would be difficult.

They started down a street, only to see five guards patrolling. They immediately melted into the shadows. It appeared that the guards had not seen them. James, the leader of the team, decided to try the next street. It appeared to be unoccupied. So they went down that street only to find out that it was being patrolled, too, after they had gone several blocks. They moved into an alley before the patrol saw them.

With repeated moving and hiding, moving and hiding they finally worked their way to the outskirts of the base before the raid started. A chained link fence blocked their way. Jonesy cut a hole in the fence with his portable torch and they made their way through, five men and three women. They were in the foot hills of the mountains and had reached safety.

The story of these eight men and women was repeated in some variation or another for thirty-one other guerillas. But all thirty-nine of the guerillas that survived the parachute drop made it to safety.

Jules and Nina succeeded in landing at the foot of the mountains as Jules intended. Jules' mission was to guide the survivors of the mission into the mountains. When they landed, Jules rolled up his chute, folded it and tied it to his back over his backpack. Nina saw what he was doing and did likewise.

CHAPTER 48
EXTRACTION

Jules and Nina were waiting at the foot of the mountain at the eastern end of the city. He and Nina laid down a covering fire for the guerillas to discourage pursuit from the Imperial troops as they went through the hole in the fence to safety. They used old fashioned automatic rifles firing bullets. One of the burglars had raided an armory and found both rifles and ammunition. He had one of the other guerillas help him carry them to the extraction point at the fence. Jules still had his cross-bow slung to his shoulder. Someone had already cut the fence when he and Nina first took up station. As soon as the guerilla troops were through the fence, Jules led them up a mountain trail.

The guerilla troops that had cut the fence themselves earlier were waiting at the bottom of the mountain trail as briefed. Jules led his band of survivors to their position, then he got the entire group started up the mountain.

They put out their flashlights and had to work their way in by moonlight at first. The trail led over a saddle in the mountain and they started down the other side. They kept traveling until morning. Before daylight, Jules found them a place to make camp. They would hide during the day.

When Jules checked over the wounded, he found that Hans had already done first aid. He cut some limbs out of drift wood and refashioned the stretchers for the ones who couldn't walk. He took the parachute from his backpack and cut it up to fasten over the tree limbs to finish up the stretchers. So they could now discard the make shift stretchers Hans had used.

When they laid down to rest, one of the assassins, Glup, looked at Nina with lust in his eyes. He'd never seen a woman so beautiful. And she looked irresistible in her tight fitting leather pants.

Exhausted, everyone went to sleep except Glup and Jules. Jules laid down his automatic rifle and took his cross-bow from his shoulder. He went seeking game so they could eat. Jules found a buck about a mile or so from camp, killed it and was dragging it back. When he was within 100 yards of the camp he heard a scream. Jules dropped the buck he was dragging and started running as fast as he could to the camp. When he got there he found Glup on top of Nina. She was fighting with all her might and Glup had blood on his face where Nina's nails had dug in.

Then Nina felt Glup go limp and collapse on top of her, blood rushing out of his throat. She felt the hot blood hit her in the face. She looked up to see Jules holding a bloody knife.

"Everyone get ready to move out," Jules commanded.

"I'm too tired to move," one of the guerillas said.

"If you stay here, you'll stay here dead," Jules said, still brandishing his bloody knife.

"Or you'll stay here dead," and he drew out his knife and lunged for Jules. Jules side stepped and cut a deep gash on Clep's forearm. Clep found he could no longer use the knife with that arm. Clep changed his knife to the other hand and lunged again. Jules side stepped while cutting a deep gash in that forearm also. Jules evaded each lunge from Clep very easily. Clep continued to bleed profusely. Finally Clep started growing weak from the loss of blood. Jules moved in and slashed his throat, severing his jugular vein. Clep fell.

"Get up and let's move out. Imperial forces will be looking for us," Jules said. Everyone got up and fell in step behind Jules. When they reached the carcass of the animal that Jules had killed, he picked it up, put if over his shoulder and continued to hurry up the trail.

At dawn Jules motioned to his troop to move off the trail and get down. His put his finger against his lips to signal silence. A squad of Imperial soldiers rushed up the trail in the direction they had come from. So they *were* looking for them!

The guerilla soldiers didn't make a sound as they saw the Imperial soldiers jog on past them. The Imperial soldiers had a wild look in their eyes. Jules waited until they were completely out of sight before he got up and motioned his troops to follow him in the opposite direction from which the Imperial soldiers had gone.

CHAPTER 49
PARATROOP DROPS

While the Fleet strike craft were pounding the base, Lieutenant Scott was sitting in a crowded landing craft, 100 miles up, near the exit ramp at the rear of his platoon. Their target: the mountain tops. Their job was to take out the gun emplacements on several of the mountain peaks. Another platoon had done a similar mission yesterday. They had covered the northern end of the mountains. That's why the fleet was briefed to keep to the north when crossing the mountains. Most of the guns had been taken out at the northern part of the mountain range by the time the strike started. But it was now time for Ben's platoon to get their piece of action. They would take up where the marines left off yesterday and take out the gun emplacements toward the center of the mountain range. Then they started descending. They descended quickly to minimize the amount of time that they would be exposed to enemy ground fire. When they were 2000 feet above the mountain peaks, they leveled off. Then the pilot maneuvered the landing craft right over the mountain tops. It was 0526 hours. Daylight would be at 0532. So it should be daylight by the time they landed.

Then the yellow light over the ramp at the front of the landing craft came on. The craft went into a hover. The exit ramp was lowered. Ben stood up. The light turned to green and Ben turned and ran down the ramp. He lit off his backpack rockets as soon as he was clear of the ship. He had a degree of control over his direction of travel if the winds aloft weren't too excessive. He had a control stick on a small control panel fastened to his belt.

While Ben and his platoon were making their jump over the mountain peaks, three other platoons were doing likewise at other locations. They were on an all out effort to capture the base. There'll be hell to pay if we don't succeed, Ben knew.

Ben guided himself to a ledge near the peak of a mountain where he had seen fire bursts from gun emplacements. He looked around. It was barely light but he could see his platoon floating down just above him. He could see the ground as it started coming up faster.

He slowed his descent and landed on the ledge as he intended. Then he unstrapped his rocket pack and discarded it. It was so heavy and bulky you couldn't fight with it on. He looked around and saw his men landing all around him. The last one to land was the platoon sergeant, as always.

He walked toward the Sergeant and said, "Any bones broken, Sarge?" He meant it in jest.

"No, sir," he said, "But I'll have to check on the men."

"Okay. Let me know when you finish checking for casualties."

In a few minutes the corpsman came up. "One man with a badly sprained ankle, and another man with a broken leg, sir." The Sergeant walked up right behind him.

"And that's all?" Ben asked.

"Did you expect more than that?" the medic asked.

"I'm not complaining about being lucky, but yes," he answered.

He turned to the sergeant, "Get the injured men under cover and make sure at least one of them has a radio. They'll be evacuated as soon as the SAR effort starts."

"Yes, sir," the sergeant answered.

They were sitting right under a anti-spacecraft gun and Ben knew it. Ben got ready to deploy his men.

"Sergeant, take Squad A around the rim of ledge to the left. Corporal Jones, you take Squad B around to the right. Get in position to knock out any guards you can see. Wait for my signal which will be one sharp blast on my whistle. Then storm the gun. Squad C, you follow me. And he took out his grappling equipment. He looked up and found a likely looking place and tossed his rope. It caught. He started climbing. When he got to the top he made the rope more secure and gave it three tugs to let the marine below him know he was ready for him to climb up.

In 15 minutes all the marines were on the upper ledge. It would be the job of the two flanking detachments to knock out the guards guarding the approaches on both sides of the gun emplacement. He and the rest of his men simply climbed over the top. He blew his whistle and then they opened fire on any enemy soldiers that they saw down below.

Within a few minutes they had taken the gun emplacement. So that was one more gun silent that the boys upstairs would appreciate. Their orders were to take the gun emplacement but not destroy it if they could hold it. They could use it themselves after they captured the planet. He had his men place charges but explained that they wouldn't fire them unless they had to abandon the gun. He deployed the platoon in the positions where they could best defend it in case of a counter attack and then sat down to wait. The first part of their mission was accomplished. Now all they had to do was wait for further orders.

CHAPTER 50
MOTHER SHIP UNDER ATTACK

When Vic arrived back at the ship he noticed the ship was still at battle quarters. He could tell because the ship's crew were still wearing their helmets. When he got back to the ready room he found out he had to get ready to man up and go back out. An enemy fleet had been detected and attack was imminent.

Vic was exhausted. And hungry. He had to wait until all the squadrons of fighter craft were launched first before he could launch again. And besides that his own ship had to be refueled and rearmed as well. So he had time to go to the wardroom and grab something to eat. Then he had to return to the ready room to brief.

At the briefing, Vic learned that two enemy spacecraft carriers were headed for them along with two cruisers and three troop ships. It was imperative that they stop them. It was very obvious that the troop transports carried troops to re-enforce the Imperial troops on the ground. The enemy probably didn't know that a major invasion force had already been landed on the planet. But the fact that they were going to try to retake the planet as soon as they found out was definitely obvious.

Vic's squadron had orders to participate in the attack on the enemy spacecraft carriers. If they could take them out it would make the rest of their job so much easier. So Vic and Ted went to the flight deck to man up.

Vic and Ted fired their strike ship out into the black goo. They formed up with the other spacecraft as a squadron and then headed for the coordinates of the last known position of the enemy fleet. All other strike squadrons on the ship had launched or were being launched. It was an all out do or die attack on the enemy's major ships.

In the briefing they had been informed that the best place to attack a major enemy space ship was at its stern. Each ship had a force field that was all but impossible to penetrate. But the main drives in the engine room generated force which interfered with the protective force field and repeated bombardment could penetrate it. Another good place to attack was, of course, the bridge. But if they could knock out the engines they'd knock out the force field making all other parts of the ship vulnerable.

After thirty minutes or so they had the enemy fleet in sight. And Vic could see swarms of enemy fighters on his EWD screen. And swarms of friendly fighters going to meet them. His objective was the major ships, carriers in particular. They took a wide berth around the air battles that the fighters were engaged in so they could get in position to attack the enemy ships from the rear. That took another half an hour or so.

Then they started their bombing runs. Torpedoes first. Man! but that ship was huge! It must have been at least 5 miles long. The squadron skipper led his flight in first, just ahead of Vic and his flight. And they had to start jinking during their run because fighters had reached them and were attacking. The skipper's four strike ships released their torpedoes and turned steeply to the left. Vic and his flight persisted until they were within range. Ted fired one torpedo, waited a count of two, then fired another. Vic turned violently to the right. Laser bursts were taking place all around them. Vic was using his "power" with all his might to avoid them. But even then there were near misses almost continuously. They flew a race track pattern to make another run. Torpedoes again.

After five torpedo runs they went in to drop their bomb load. This was a little more complicated. They had to get in closer and Vic had to pull up steeply as soon as Ted released their bombs.

Then it was time to return to the mother ship. They were out of ordnance except for their laser cannon that they used for self defense against fighter craft. And they were low on fuel. En route, the squadron skipper had them check in. Out of twenty-four strike craft, only eight were left!

They arrived back at the mother ship and maneuvered into the landing docks. Vic set his ship down and secured the engines. He and Ted completed the shutdown checklist and headed for the ready room to debrief. He told the deck crew to refuel and rearm for a quick turnaround. They arrived back at the ready room for the end of flight debrief. The squadron skipper was there. Looking very haggard and tired. Just like Vic felt.

"Get down to the wardroom and eat while your ships are being refueled and armed. We'll launch again at 0200 hours." Then following his own advice he headed down the passageway to the wardroom, himself.

* * *

The battle raged for over 25 hours. Vic learned later that they did destroy one of the carriers and severely damaged the other. There were clumps of wreckage splattered throughout the combat area from the remnants of destroyed fighters and strike spacecraft. Finally the battle was over. Exhausted, Vic fell into his bunk.

CHAPTER 51
HIT AGAIN

Vic checked the flight schedule to find that they had another strike on the main base of the planet scheduled for the next night. The enemy would have figured out by now that they were not coming from the same direction each time. So if they came in from a new direction again it would be either north or south. But they wouldn't know which. So the decision was made to enter the planet's atmosphere 5,000 miles to the south of their target over the ocean. And then fly to the target, skimming the waves, as usual. They arrived at their destination at about 0600 hours. The defenders of the base still either managed advanced warning, or they just guessed when and where they would be because the fighter aircraft were airborne when they arrived and launched a massive attack against them as soon as they got near. The strike spacecraft started jinking and shooting and naturally all their friendly fighters engaged them as soon as possible.

They had succeeded in the destruction of the launch pads the previous day. But they must have had construction crews working continuously since then to repair them. They repaired enough of them to get quite a few fighter craft in the air.

On his first bombing run, Vic had jinked hard to the right to avoid a laser burst when he received a solid hit. He was pointed toward the mountains with the nose of his spacecraft pointed slightly up. He tried maneuvering and found out he'd lost directional control.

"Get ready to eject," he told Ted over the intercom. So they both tightened their straps and pulled the visors down on their helmets and hit the eject button. And just in time because the spacecraft flew straight into the mountain and exploded in a fireball.

Vic's backpack rocket fired off automatically as it should, so he reached down for the control stick fastened to his waist to guide himself to a landing spot. He looked over to the right and saw Ted so he made it out okay, too. They were right at the peak of the middle of the mountain range. Vic saw a shelf and headed for it. He eased himself down and landed. He looked over and saw Ted set down near him.

There were two different eject buttons. One would fire an ejection capsule which is the one they used in outer space. The other would shoot you out of the capsule. This was the one for use if you were near the ground. You'd still have on your pressure suit.

Vic and Ted both shed their pressure suits as rapidly as they could. Vic figured the first thing to do was to just find a place to hole up. Avoid being seen. There would be no SAR spacecraft looking for them while the base was still in enemy hands. And if captured, and identified as a former officer of the Old Empire, he'd be tried and shot for treason and desertion. That he knew. So he and Ted discarded their rocket packs and started looking for a likely hiding place.

He and Ted found shelter among some rocks. They were exhausted so it was a relief to just get to rest awhile. They decided to sleep in turns. Vic took the first watch. After a couple of hours, Ted relieved him. He told Ted to wake him in two hours. It was full daylight by now.

Ted woke him after two hours. He felt like he had just barely closed his eyes. They were both red-eyed with fatigue. But he forgot the fatigue within seconds. Enemy soldiers were walking the mountain ridge toward them from the north! So they started out walking south. They knew it would be easy to fall and break a leg or worse since neither of them had spent very much time in the mountains. But they'd have to just do the best they could. Then they saw troops headed toward them from the south. They already knew the west side of the ridge was almost straight down so they turned and started working their way across the mountain peak to the east. When they got to the end of a ledge and looked down they saw that side was straight down, too. For a couple of thousand feet, at least.

So Vic went back to the peak of the mountain and started looking for a place that would be fairly easy to defend. They'd be killed, but at least they could make their death as dear as possible to the enemy.

Vic found a place and he and Ted climbed behind some rocks. The troops on the north were closer so he figured they'd reach them first. Nothing to do now but wait.

When the Imperial troops were within about 100 yards they saw Vic and Ted. The enemy soldiers sought cover and started firing. They were out of range of the blast pistols that Vic and Ted were carrying. So they just kept down. The enemy soldiers apparently knew their probable location but maybe they hadn't pinpointed their exact position, yet.

After a few minutes, he saw the troops in their black uniforms leave their hiding places and move toward them for about 20 yards or so then disappear behind rocks again. After a few seconds they did so again. It seemed like they thought they were going up against a major armed force. The next time they jumped up and ran toward them they got within 50 yards so. Vic opened fire. He saw two of them fall to his blast pistol before they found cover behind the rocks again.

Vic looked over at Ted and saw he had a light saber in his left hand. It was better than a blast pistol at close quarters. He had been carrying it with his survival gear. Ted was left handed. His blast pistol was in his right hand. Vic thought about how he should include his light saber in his survival gear. He had one that he kept in his quarters at the mother ship. He just didn't think he'd ever need it while flying.

Then a shot bounced off the rock right in front of Ted. It had come from behind them. Vic turned to see four enemy soldiers within 30 feet of them. He turned and shot two of them. Ted got one. The other made it to the nest in the rocks they were defending. Ted cut off his head with his light saber. Vic turned back to the front and continued firing at the attackers storming the position from the front. He told Ted to cover the rear while he continued fighting the men coming from the front.

Then they heard yells coming from behind the attacking soldiers toward the north. The soldiers in black uniforms turned and started firing toward their rear. Then the enemy soldiers turned back toward Vic and Ted and started running. They had apparently forgotten all about Vic and Ted and just ran past them. Then Vic saw Fleet Marines chasing them. They had the enemy in full rout!

It appeared the enemy position was completely over run and the Imperial troops were in full retreat.

Then Vic saw a Fleet Marine. He immediately stood and held his hands high. The marine very quickly covered him with his blast rifle.

He looked over to his left and found that Ted had followed suit.

"We're downed Fleet pilots," Vic explained.

"Advance and be recognized but come slow," one of the marines ordered. He appeared to be a non-com. Vic and Ted did so, still holding their arms high above their heads.

The non-com turned to one of the marines and said, "Take them back to the Lieutenant. Let him decide what to do with them."

The squad of enemy soldiers that had been approaching from the south were obviously in full retreat, as well. The marine took them back to the platoon commander. Then Vic recognized him. Ben Scott!

"You sure are a sight for sore eyes!" Vic exclaimed. Ben grinned from ear to ear and changed his blast rifle to his left hand so he could wring Vic's hand with his right. Then Vic introduced him to Ted and he shook hands with him.

"Just stay behind us but do your best to keep up. We want to catch these guys and mop them up, if possible."

Three hours later, Vic felt the vibrator go off on his communicator. That meant that SAR aircraft were searching for them! Ben explained later that the acting base commander had surrendered the base at about midmorning. During the night all the senior officers on the base had been killed in their beds by guerilla soldiers while asleep. With all their senior officers dead, there was no other alternative.

The SAR spacecraft landed and picked up Vic and Ted on a shelf of the mountain and they headed back to the mother ship.

Chapter 52
Army Tanks and Infantry

General Wup, commander of the Army Troops for the New Empire, received orders from the Task Force Commander to start landing his tank and infantry forces. One troop transport started its descent. Its destination was the desert closest to the main base on the planet. The second transport went to another continent where an advanced base was located. The third one to a third continent. The planet Astro had been rather lightly defended by the Imperial Fleet. That's why the admirals of the New Empire chose it as their first target. Their attack had the element of surprise going for it from the beginning. The main base was now in the hands of the New Empire so the enemy's main source of communication with its senior commanders had been cut off.

The tank ships landed in the desert to unload their tanks and personnel carriers. There they organized their regiment. The space port was being repaired so they could land infantry troops at the space port for the main base. Infantry troops and personnel carriers were also landed to back up the tank battalions. Once the tanks and trucks were free of the transport ship they raised up above the ground high enough not to stir up the sand and started moving into position. They formed a battle line where they could move either way depending on the direction of any attacking forces.

Similar activities were going on at each continent of the planet. Within a week the entire planet had been taken and occupied. Now they started building up their defenses in preparation for a counter-attack from Imperial forces that they knew would come. The enemy anti-spacecraft gun facilities were being repaired. As were bunkers and early warning detection gear. The idea of using the enemy's own guns against them appealed to the troops of the New Empire. It would be giving them a taste of their own medicine in the literal sense. Hoards of prisoners had been captured and were being herded into make shift prisoner of war camps. They would be fed and given medical attention as needed until there was time to interview them for prospective defectors. They needed to beef up their own ranks with new recruits.

Word was passed to prepare for a counter attack from outer space. So men were working around the clock to repair anti-air weapons and get tanks and artillery pieces in place. The infantry were deployed and ordered to dig in and get ready for an attack. General Wup was just glad that they had managed to take and occupy the planet before the Imperial re-enforcements arrived. It was much easier to defend ground already taken than to take it to begin with.

* * *

The Old Empire immediately dispatched two spacecraft carriers with additional support ships as needed as soon as they found out that Astro was under attack. They were three weeks away from Astro when they first received orders to go to Astro with great haste.

After three weeks they approached Astro only to find three enemy spacecraft carriers and large amounts of Rebel troops already on the ground on Astro fighting the Imperial forces.

It was obvious that the first thing to do would be to take out the enemy carriers first. There was a third Imperial carrier coming but it would take it another week to reach this area. So Admiral Gup's decision was to attack the Rebel carriers now, in spite of going against superior numbers.

So he launched all his strike craft against the New Empire carriers with all the fighter cover he could give them. He saw swarms of fighter craft launching from the Rebel carriers coming to meet them. Then he saw Rebel strike craft heading for the Imperial carriers. A major battle was apparently in the making.

The fighters engaged and a fierce space battle developed very quickly. You could see laser bursts everywhere as fighter ships exploded. It turned into mass confusion. All the spacecraft that were space worthy had been launched from Vic's ship. Vic found out he had to use the "power" for all he was worth picking out targets on his detection gear and jinking radically to avoid getting hit.

From a distance it would have looked like a tangle of red wires with red and yellow blobs bursting throughout the mass of wire periodically.

CHAPTER 53
REINFORCEMENTS

During the twenty-five hour space battle just recounted, Admiral Genski had sent the troop transports under fighter cover on down to the planet to land. He had managed to keep all the Rebel forces' attention focused on the space battle in the vicinity of the Imperial Fleet. The loss of one spacecraft carrier he could ill afford. And the other was damaged, though they could still launch and recover spacecraft from it.

He decided he'd better re-enforce the troops on the ground as soon as possible. He didn't know that the Rebel forces had already taken and occupied the entire planet and that the forces on the ground were already prisoners of war. But he was soon to learn this. The landing craft had to face horrendous anti-spaceship fire on the way down to land and when they landed they found resistance from ground infantry forces formidable.

When they sent down the tank and personnel carrier landing craft, they found out that they had Rebel tanks and infantry with anti-tank guns on the ground to meet them. Many of the vehicles were destroyed while attempting to exit the landing craft.

So they found out they were making an invasion against heavy enemy forces rather than just re-enforcing their troops. In fact, they didn't see any of their own troops.

They succeeded in getting enough men and equipment on the planet to establish a battle line on one continent. They'd have to take that continent before they could try to expand their position beyond that. And that was going to be a formidable undertaking. But fighting was their stock in trade so they set out to dig in and build a battle line. The tanks all formed up and prepared to launch an attack against the Rebel troops and the infantry dug in, taking their positions behind the tank forces. They dug their fox holes in the soft sand. Personnel carriers were brought up and made ready in case it became possible to make any advances against the enemy.

As the day wore on, the desert got hot. The tank crews were sweating in their tanks. The infantry were sweating in their fox holes. Just waiting. What a soldier hates to do more than anything else and what he has to spend more time doing than anything else. Waiting.

At night fall the word was passed that they'd attack at dawn the following morning. To get ready. The men got ready to roll up in their blankets and men were posted to guard duty.

They kicked off at dawn as planned. They found resistance very stiff but they saw they had the Rebel troops between their own forces and the sea. The General in command of the Imperial forces thought he should be able to take them easily.

The tanks rolled out, firing at the enemy forces. Anti-tank fire started bursting among the tanks. A tank blew up every few minutes. The infantry officers started moving their men out of their fox holes and getting them ready to move forward and take any ground the tanks gained. And General Genski ordered the battalions to spread out so he could cover both the enemy's flanks.

It seemed like the enemy Rebels would have to surrender or be driven into the sea.

CHAPTER 54
CLOSE AIR SUPPORT

After six hours of sleep, Vic got up and went to the ready room to see when he was scheduled to fly again. In two hours. He went to the wardroom to eat and then back to the ready room to brief. He learned the enemy had succeeded in landing troops on the planet surface and that the ground troops needed air support. So they would be flying close air support missions today.

At the briefing Vic and Ted learned that the main base had surrendered and they had 10,000 prisoners to handle. But at an auxiliary base about 1,000 miles to the southeast of the main base Imperial troops had landed during the night. That was where the close air support was needed. It was a position being defended by the Army of the New Empire.

They launched, only two squadrons this time. Since this planet was intended as an advanced base for the New Empire for future operations they wanted to minimize the damage to the defense facilities on the base. They would be targeting enemy ground troops this time.

They came in low from the south so they could approach over the ocean. Vic was leading his flight of four spacecraft and he came in first. They found the enemy ground forces and started making strafing runs. And making laser shots at enemy tanks and personnel carriers.

After three runs and no losses of their strike spacecraft they left and headed back to outer space. Other strike flights were still pounding the enemy soldiers on the ground. Vic's flight was attacked by enemy fighters on the way back to the mother ship. Vic's "power" instincts stood him in good stead again. He was able to jink just in time to avoid any hits from enemy fighters and downed two of them himself.

Randell K. Whaley

* * *

Five thousand Imperial soldiers had been landed at the Auxiliary Base at Rocky Point. They formed a battle line in a semi-circle and were trying to take Rocky Point back from the New Empire Army troops. The New Empire forces had managed to fortify their position but they were between the enemy and the sea. So it appeared they were surrounded and placed under siege. The New Empire forces weren't to know yet that the space battle had gone in their favor and that the sources of supply for the Imperial Army had been, for all practical purposes cut off. For now they just knew their own forces needed help. So General Wup had sent a message to the main headquarters that he needed re-enforcements. They arrived in the form of Fleet Marines. It was decided that at least two battalions of Fleet Marines could be spared.

So the 10th Battalion and the 15th Battalion of the 5th Regiment of the Fleet Marines was loaded into landing craft and rushed across the continent to Rocky Point. They landed on the desert side so they could attack the enemy from their rear. Ben's platoon was among them.

While Ben's platoon was engaging the enemy, Vic and Ted were making their strafing runs against the enemy lines. The enemy troops were fighting desperately. Their commanders had probably already tried to radio for re-enforcements and most likely already knew they weren't coming. Of course, Vic and Ted knew they had destroyed a considerable portion of the enemy task force in the space battle. This was really a mop up operation. Unless the Old Empire succeeded in getting more re-enforcements to the area.

The Old Empire was rushing more re-enforcements to the area but it would be another week before they arrived. So it was imperative that they subdue the Imperial troops currently on the ground between now and then.

Vic was moving his spacecraft low over the enemy forces and strafing the ground thoroughly for maximum effect. Enemy small arms fire was bouncing off his spacecraft continuously but his defensive shield was holding and no damage was being done.

Now Fleet Marines were trained as assault troops. They weren't trained like the Army troops for a long land campaign. Their tactics were to rush the enemy and overwhelm them as soon as possible. Their two battalions with a total of 500 men were going against 5,000 enemy soldiers. They had the enemy troops in a squeeze. New Empire Army troops were fighting them from the west while the Marines were attacking them from the east. But Ben just threw his men into battle vigorously like he had been trained to do and like had always been successful in the past. After all they were attacking in full force with 500 men.

But the commander of the Battalion in which Ben's platoon was a part made a misjudgment. He didn't watch his flanks. Very soon his men were surrounded and fighting for their lives. He immediately took his radio and called for an air strike. Vic recognized Ben's voice on the radio.

"Light Saber Two on the way," he called so that the squadron commander would hear him. He maneuvered his spacecraft to the coordinates that Ben had given him. He made a low strafing run and saw bodies flying everywhere under the intensity of the spray of laser fire he laid on the ground. He saw the Fleet Marines totally surrounded with enemy troops. After he passed them, he pulled his nose up and brought his spacecraft to a sudden stop, reversed course and brought it back down to make another strafing run on the east side of Ben's position. Sand flew and bodies were flying everywhere again.

But Vic could see it was no use. Ben's platoon was being overwhelmed. He'd have to land and extract them.

"Light Saber Two landing to extract a platoon," he said over the radio.

"Light Saber Two get out of there!" yelled the squadron commander over the radio. "Don't land! I repeat don't land!"

Vic reached over and turned his radio off. "We just had a radio failure," he said to Ted over the intercom. Ted looked toward him and nodded with a knowing look on his face. Vic set the spacecraft down in the sand as close as he could to Ben's position. Ted was out of his seat and had the hatch open and the ladder down by the time Vic had set the spacecraft engines on idle. Vic followed him. Vic had remembered his experience the last time he and Ted had found themselves on the ground. He had brought his light saber along this time. They rushed down the ladder with light sabers drawn. Vic had his blast pistol in his left hand. Ted held his blast pistol in his right and his light saber in his left as before.

"Get your men aboard," Vic yelled to Ben.

"Get aboard," Ben in turned yelled to the ragged survivors of his platoon, "Wounded men first."

Two marines were hauled aboard on stretchers. Four more marines followed them, a couple of them limping badly. Imperial soldiers were rushing them from two sides. Vic got the first one on the side of the head and he went down. Two more went down to his light saber immediately afterward.

"You, too," Vic yelled to Ben.

"No way," Ben answered. He had his light saber out and was fighting beside Vic. Four marines piled out of the spacecraft and engaged the enemy with their blast rifles. Their blast rifles each had an electric bayonet that would sever an enemy head just with a single stroke. They fought with such ferocity that within minutes there was a lull in the fighting. The ground was strewn with corpses.

"Now get them inside the spacecraft. And yourself, too," Vic yelled. This time Ben did so. Vic motioned to Ted to get inside, too. Then he followed. He jumped into the pilot's seat and moved the ship off the ground as rapidly as he could.

"Get the ladder up and the hatch closed," Vic told Ted. Ted got out of his seat to do so. He still had his blast pistol in his right hand. An Imperial soldier was climbing the ladder even though they were a good hundred feet in the air. Ted shot him with his blast pistol and saw him turn loose of the ladder and fall. Then he retrieved the ladder, closed the outer hatch, then the inner hatch. He returned to the Bombardier seat and strapped in. Vic had fastened his seat straps by this time. He set the ship for maximum power straight up.

When they were clear of the planet's atmosphere, Ted set the coordinates of the mother ship into the navigational computer and it provided Vic a heading to fly to the spacecraft carrier.

When they were in outer space and clear of any fighting, Vic called the mother ship on the radio and notified them that they had wounded men aboard. They'd need medical personal on hand when they landed.

All the other spacecraft in the squadron had already landed. Vic eased the ship into the landing bay and sat her down on the deck as gently as he could. Two of the marines in the back handed down the two stretcher cases to waiting corpsmen first. Then the rest of the marines disembarked. Then Ted went down the ladder. Vic was last, as was the custom for the pilot in command of a ship.

"Squadron Commander wants to see you in his office," came a message from a spacer.

"Okay," replied Vic.

He made his way to the Squadron Commander's office. He walked in and stood at attention.

"Why did you land against orders?" the Squadron Commander almost screamed.

"I heard no such order, sir," Vic had a look of total innocence on his face. Serious and stern but was careful not to let any guilt show.

"I gave you specific orders not to land but to get out of there. You endangered your Bombardier and spacecraft against orders." The Squadron Commander was still almost screaming.

"I must have been in a blind spot, sir," Vic answered in as humble a voice as he could muster. "I did not hear your order on the radio." It is possible to have temporary interruption in radio reception due to the concept of a "blind spot." But that was normally if you had a mountain or something similar between you and the location you were trying to send to or receive from, which was not the case this time, of course.

"So you did not hear my order," the Squadron CO was starting to calm down a little by now. "How many men did you rescue?" he asked.

"Seven Fleet Marines, sir, four of them wounded."

The Squadron CO knew that a court martial would throw the case out due to lack of evidence if he couldn't prove that Vic heard the order. He knew Vic was lying but couldn't prove it.

"And the wounded men?"

"They're in sick bay, sir," Vic answered. All of the marines had reported to sick bay to see if they had any injuries they weren't aware of.

The squadron commander paused a moment and then said, "Dismissed."

Vic immediately went to sick bay to check on Ben. When he arrived he saw Ben in a hospital bed with a big bandage on his thigh.

"So you were wounded and were fighting like that," Vic mused.

"Just a flesh wound. Didn't keep me from moving around."

"It certainly didn't," Vic confirmed. "You move mighty fast for a wounded marine."

"Thanks. We're even, now," Ben said with a grin and held out his hand.

Vic took his hand with both his hands and smiled back. "Glad you made it. And glad we managed to save the last of your platoon." Ben had started with 35 men. Only 6 had survived besides himself.

CHAPTER 55
CAMPAIGN DRAWS TO AN END

So there was finally a lull in the fighting. Vic and Ted noticed they were hungry. They hadn't noticed before. So they went to the wardroom for chow. They could have chow at the combat pilot's wardroom any time of the day or night because of the varying nature of their flight schedule. So they could eat when they got the chance between flights. After they ate, they went to their respective staterooms to sack out. Vic almost fell asleep on his feet while walking to his stateroom. He fell into his bunk and slept for 12 hours. The squadron commander had issued orders to allow the combat crews to sleep as long as they wanted. Now that the battle was over he wanted his pilots to rest up.

Vic continued to send messages to Red every day or two. He missed her more than ever now that the war was winding down. He now had the time to miss her. There wasn't much time to think of anything but the job at hand when the fighting is hot and heavy. They got down to just flying patrols. The screen for the mother ship was done by fighter craft, but they used strike spacecraft for patrolling the area they'd taken on the planet itself. And they were alert for reprisals from other quadrants. If the Old Empire had the forces, it would stand to reason that they'd try to regain the base they'd just lost. But in the meantime, they just flew their patrols and made sure everything was secure.

They did receive word that two more carriers had arrived from the Old Empire and all the fighter craft were scrambled to meet them. Vic and Ted reported to the ready room in flight gear ready for a strike. The CO told them to just hang around in the ready room. The fighters were being scrambled. They didn't have orders to launch strike spacecraft, yet.

The Old Empire had a couple of other wars going on, Vic knew. The Admiral had picked a time when the Old Empire was engaged in a major campaign with another enemy before starting the attack on Astro. It turned out that the enemy forces withdrew and didn't renew their attack. The New Empire had consolidated their positions and refurbished the battered defenses and would be very, very hard to overcome by now.

After about a month Vic found out he had received orders to detach from his squadron and transfer down to the planet surface. Something to do with interviewing prisoners. Now he'd never been connected with intelligence. Nor did he want to be. So he didn't understand that. He checked with his squadron commander. Commander Jacks explained that he was aware of his orders and that he didn't want to lose him as a strike pilot. But he was one of the very few officers in the Fleet that had the "power." They were screening the prisoners for defectors to beef up their own forces.

Okay. So Vic understood now, and it made perfect sense. So within a few days he found himself sitting in an office. Two guards would usher in a prisoner. And from behind his desk, Vic would "look right through him" and find out if he was still loyal to the Old Empire or if he wished to join the New Empire and fight for freedom. He wasn't surprised at the number of them that chose to defect. Most of the ones that didn't were men with families back on the planet Armenia. He could understand how they wouldn't want to come over to the Fleet. They'd not only never see their families again, but reprisals might be made against them. However, two out of three of the young, unmarried men were more than willing to defect to a cause that had some hope of a happy future.

They had to interview 14,000 prisoners. Vic learned that there were about a dozen officers in the Fleet that had the "power." And Vic found out he could interview about 60 to 70 prisoners a day. Each one that passed an interview were issued New Empire uniforms and sworn into the fleet.

Then a man in buckskin clothing and moccasins walked in with a woman walking beside him dressed in snug fitting leather pants and a faded jersey. A guard walked in and explained, "These two aren't prisoners but insisted on seeing you."

Vic looked at them. Both had on rough clothing but were clean. "Yes?" Vic queried.

"We want to remain on this planet," Jules explained.

"Why do you ask me that?" Vic returned.

"We are members of the guerilla troop that attacked and assassinated the senior Imperial officers the night before the base was surrendered to New Empire forces. I'd like the guerillas to be accepted as citizens of this planet." He didn't say sir. He apparently was not accustomed to recognizing authority in anyone other than himself.

"Do you wish to join the Fleet?" Vic asked.

"No sir, but some of the guerrillas might. They'd make good Fleet Marines, sir." He said sir, this time. That was unusual.

"You'll have to let them come in for an interview, one at a time," Vic explained.

So the guerrilla troops were granted the opportunity to join either the Fleet or Fleet Marines if they passed their interview. The ones that were bonafide criminals, of course, didn't pass their interview. Many, maybe even most of the "criminals" from the Old Empire were actually just victims of circumstances fighting for their own rights.

Jules and Nina went back to the mountains and Jules started building them a cabin. He planned to resume his career as a trapper and mountain man.

After about two months, the interviewing of prisoners had been accomplished for the most part. So Vic learned he was to be transferred back to his squadron on the mother ship. He requested 30 days leave.

* * *

When Vic arrived at Ultaria, Red met him at the spaceport, of course. Her tummy was bulging out really good by now. He knew she would be about 8 ½ months along. He was overcome with awe from her beauty as usual, this time even more so because of the "contented look" on her face. She walked up to him to hug him and he grabbed her by the shoulders and gently turned her sideways to hug her and gave her a big kiss. "Mustn't squeeze little tyke," he murmured in her ear.

"I know," she whispered back.

They went to the luggage reclaim area to retrieve Vic's luggage. After picking up his luggage, they went out to where the red saucer was parked. Vic pulled up the door to the luggage compartment in the back and put his luggage in place. After closing the luggage hatch, he opened the hatch to the cockpit and helped Red inside. A little cramped with her expanded size. And Vic was really careful on take-off and flew the saucer as smoothly as he could.

CHAPTER 56
NEW BABY!

At dawn, Red started groaning. It woke Vic up. He immediately called the midwife on the video/audio machine. She was there in 15 minutes. Jenny, her helper, and two Fleet corpsmen were in attendance. And the corpsmen weren't part of the midwife's clinic. The Admiral had apparently given the midwife instructions to call the hospital as soon as Red went into labor.

Red had flat refused to have a doctor in attendance. "They're not giving me drugs, certainly not while the baby's still attached to my umbilical cord," she had said very vehemently. Now, the Admiral outranked everyone on 137 planets. Or 138 planets now since they had just recently added another. But he apparently didn't outrank his daughter. He had obviously sent the two corpsmen over anyway, apparently without her permission. She accepted that. They couldn't give her drugs at least. She knew a medical doctor would insist on giving her drugs and she knew she'd be in no shape to fight him over it.

The midwife put on her surgical gloves, took her electric shaver and started prepping Red. Red was still groaning and writhing in agony. Vic just stood off to the side. He appreciated being allowed in attendance but he figured maybe the best thing he could do would be to stay out of the way.

"Go hold her hand," the midwife said with her lips only. Vic saw her lip movement so he walked over to Red's bedside and took her hand. Her eyes were closed so she didn't see him but when she felt his hand she grabbed it with both of hers and he wondered if she was going to squeeze it in two. Then she screamed, a loud blood curdling scream. Vic felt terrified. He had no idea what to do. He'd never been this scared in his life. He'd rather face 10 enemy fighter pilots than face what he was facing, now.

Red relaxed again but in 10 seconds she was writhing in agony again. In the corner of his eye, he saw the midwife pushing against Red's upper belly. Then in between groans Red tried to say something. Vic said, "Yes?"

She mumbled some more, groaned, then mumbled some more. "Go watch the baby get born," came out finally, barely audible, and she released his hand.

So Vic stepped back. The baby's head was out. Mary, the midwife, was waiting for the shoulders to show so she'd have something to grip. Finally the shoulders appeared. So Mary gripped the baby's little shoulders and just gently started pulling. Very, very slowly. No hurry. He heard Red grunting but the screaming and groaning had stopped. Then Mary finished pulling the baby out. She placed her on a small side bench that she had brought in and sat up when she first arrived and Jenny handed her the string and scissors. She tied off the umbilical cord in two places about an inch apart, and then cut it in two. Then she went back to massage Red's belly. Jenny took a sponge and started rubbing the baby down. Then after she'd had her first bath, she dried her off with what looked like a very soft towel. Then she put a diaper on her, wrapped her in a blanket and then picked her up. She just systematically handed her to Vic as if that was what she was supposed to do next.

Vic was awestruck. He just held the tiny little thing and looked at her. He'd never seen anything so beautiful before. And she opened up her little eyes and just stared at him. Vic knew that a newborn baby's eyes can't focus, yet, but this little girl was sure trying her best. And she had red hair. Just like her mom. And she had a pretty good head of hair for a newborn. He stroked her little head. Her hair was so soft! Then his attention was drawn to the fact that the midwife and corpsman were arranging the bed sheets over Red's legs.

"She's good as new," she nodded to Vic. "Now hand her the baby so she can feed it." "Turn over on your side honey, so you can feed little one," she told Red.

Red did so. Vic noticed how tired she looked. The fatigue really showed on her face. In fact, she looked completely worn out. But she offered a breast to little Miriam. Little Miriam didn't want it. It's like as if she was thinking, who's trying to pry my mouth open?

Then Red squirted some milk on her little mouth. She opened her mouth to lick it off and must have decided it tasted pretty good. So she took the nipple then with no problem and started her first meal. Once she got going she really ate with an appetite.

Mary was gathering her stuff and getting ready to go. Vic followed her to the living room. He said, "She didn't cry?" He just wondered why.

"They don't always cry. I saw her take a deep breath as soon as she came out so I knew she was okay. Babies don't always cry when they're born."

She finished packing her gear and she and Jenny left. She said she had another baby to deliver across town. The mother was already in labor. The two corpsmen hung around. Vic walked back into the bedroom. Red was burping the baby, getting ready to roll over to the other side to give her the other breast.

"Hungry?" Vic asked.

"No, I'm exhausted," she replied.

"If I brought you some food would you eat it?"

"Whatever you say," was her answer.

Vic went to the kitchen to fix some breakfast and found out that one of the corpsmen already had food on the stove cooking. When he saw Vic walk in he handed him a cup of hot herbal tea he'd already made. So Vic took her the tea and got her to take a couple of sips of it. He decided to make sure she had something to eat before she went to sleep. When she'd finished feeding the baby he reached down and picked the little one up.

The corpsman came in from the kitchen with some toast and porridge on a tray. He placed it on the bedside table where she could reach it. Vic just held the littlest lady. Spitting image of her mother he noticed again as he gazed at her little face. Her eyes were closed, now. After a full tummy she just promptly went to sleep. Her mama ate maybe half her breakfast and she promptly went to sleep, too.

* * *

Two days later Mary paid Red a visit. She wanted to check on Red and the baby, of course, but she'd managed to catch up on her paper work and brought the baby's birth certificate. Vic looked at the time of birth. 6:46 AM. Red had woke up in labor at 6:02 AM. It only took 44 minutes from the time her labor pains started. It had seemed like hours. Vic asked her how much he owed her and paid her before she left.

Vic was glad *that* was over with. But he sure was proud of their new little family member.

CHAPTER 57
DAN VISITS MYRNA

Dan was out at the corral practicing with his rope. He had decided to spend his 30 days leave with Myrna on her ranch. And he had decided to learn to be a cowboy. He was told by Cal, the one cowboy that could speak Ultarian, that to be a cowboy he'd have to learn to handle a rope. He and Myrna had ridden down to the herd that one time and watched the cowboys branding cattle. And he saw how one cowboy would rope a calf while another cowboy roped its mother and then another cowboy would throw the calf and hold it down while a fourth cowboy brought a branding iron from the fire and branded it. So he understood how roping would be a basic skill for a cowboy.

And it was much harder than it looked. He was attempting to rope a post out in the corner of the corral and it seemed to move every time he tossed his loop toward it.

"Relax. You're too tense," Cal told him.

"Oh. Is that what I'm doing wrong?"

"Only one 'em. Let me show you how to do it again," Cal suggested.

Dan watched the loop settle over the post like as if it was the easiest thing to do in the world.

In the corner of his eye he saw Myrna walk up. "It's time for lunch," she said.

"That is a good idea," he answered. He coiled up the rope and hung it on a corral post. Then he started walking toward the ranch house with Myrna beside him. After lunch they went riding again. They went riding every afternoon. Hal roped his horse for him but Dan saddled him. He had already learned to do that. Hal saddled Myrna's horse. She didn't saddle her own.

After they had ridden for a couple of hours they came to a brook and Myrna stopped and dismounted. Dan followed suit. Myrna found a log to sit on and Dan sat down beside her.

"One thing I should tell you," she said. "Even though we no longer have rustlers stealing cattle I still am having problems making the ranch pay. It looks like I'll have to make another loan at the bank to meet expenses this year."

"Hmmm," Dan said. "How much of your ranch have I seen?"

"A small part of it."

"Could you take me around to look at the rest of it?"

"Yes, but not all in one day. It's too big."

"It would be good if I had a better idea of your operation. I might be able to come up with an idea or two about how to improve profits," he said.

"Do you think you could?" She didn't say that her late husband would have thought of something though that was what she was thinking.

"Yes," was his answer.

They remounted and continued riding. But this time Dan started looking for clues about how the ranch was being operating. He knew a ranch this big should be making a good profit.

It took several days to finally tour the entire ranch. Then Dan asked her if he could see her books. He explained that he was good with numbers. She agreed.

He spent half a day looking over the accounting records for the ranch. Then over lunch he said, "I notice you spend a lot of money on hay during the winters."

"Yes, when there's snow on the ground, the cattle would have nothing to eat otherwise.

"We rode through that one valley that had really tall grass, rich and green."

"That was near the mountain. We get more rain in that valley than anywhere else."

"If you could cut hay and store it for the winter you wouldn't have to buy hay," he mentioned.

"Yes, but cowboys are specialists. They would take it as an insult if you expected them to do work an ordinary farm hand would do."

"You could hire farm hands to come in and cut the hay, bale it and haul it to your barns," he suggested.

"I hadn't thought of that!" And she brightened up at the idea.

"Has mowing equipment been invented yet on this planet?"

"Yes. I can buy a horse drawn mower and they also have horse drawn baling machines." Dan suggested they take a trip to town and look at farm equipment and see her banker about borrowing the money to buy haying machines. The grass was ready to mow now. They'd just need to hire some farm hands and get them started making hay.

Within two days they had hay hands out in the valley cutting hay. Dan found out that the mower produced a windrow of hay behind the mowing machine. The baler followed the mowing machine producing bales that weighed probably 60 or 70 pounds. Myrna already had the horses she needed to pull the implements. She kept work horses to pull wagons and buckboards with. So all she had to buy was the two machines.

CHAPTER 58
PLANET SIDE DUTY

Vic got new orders before his 30 days leave was up. He found out he had been transferred to the space flight training command. As an instructor for fighter craft. This was good news. And he had a sneaky feeling the Admiral might have exerted an influence here. But he certainly wasn't complaining. He definitely wanted to spend some time with his wife and new daughter. And he was very, very tired of war.

His students were the rank rookies that had never been in any kind of spacecraft except maybe transports. In fact, a lot of them were recruited from the prisoners of war taken on Astro. He took them up and had them practice take offs and landings first, of course. They had been through ground school and had simulator training already. And he couldn't believe how totally unaware of anything the young student pilots were. It was like dealing with babies. So it required some adjustment in his own thinking. They had to start learning from somewhere and it seemed like for most of them, somewhere was nowhere. But he learned patience. He had to learn patience or lose his mind, he found out.

So he now had an 8 hour a day job, and was home for dinner every night. When he landed the little red saucer in the back yard of their house and came in the back door, the first thing he did, of course, was give Red a hug and kiss. But the next thing he would always do was check on his little girl. Sometimes she'd be sleeping, sometimes she'd be lying awake in her little crib. If she was laying awake, he'd always pick her up and hold her and talk to her a few minutes. And as soon as control of her little facial muscles developed, it got so she always smiled every time she saw her daddy.

* * *

And he was happy to be able to notify Red that had a new promotion, to Full Lieutenant, O-3.

CHAPTER 59
GRANDPA

The Admiral saw his new grandchild for the first time the next day after she was born. He was flanked by two aides. They always accompanied him wherever he went. He walked into the living room to find Vic holding her. She was kicking and waving her little arms. Getting her work out. As soon as Vic saw the Admiral he came to attention. Not to full attention. The little bundle was still in his arms. Then he walked over and handed the Admiral his new granddaughter. At first the Admiral acted like he didn't know what to do. It was the first time he'd ever seen the Admiral in other than his stiff, commanding Fleet Admiral roll.

But the Admiral just held her and looked at her little face. She stared at him with her eyes open wide and kept on staring. It was like as if she wanted to memorize every feature of his face. He found out they had named her Miriam.

* * *

Two weeks later, at her christening ceremony, the Admiral walked up to Vic and said, "So you deliberately made her a girl."

Vic just said, "Yes, sir." He knew he couldn't hide anything from the Admiral. You can't hide something from a mind reader.

"And you knew I wanted a grandson."

Vic just said, "Yes, sir," again.

"You knew that Red secretly wanted a daughter and told no one about it, even you."

Vic just said, "Yes, sir," again.

"And you can overdo the sirring, son," he added.

"Yes, sir," was all Vic could think of to say.

The Admiral walked over to Red who was holding little Miriam and held out his hands. Her mother took the cue and handed her to him. Then he carried her back to where Vic was standing. "She is really a beautiful girl."

Vic could only say, "Yes, sir. Like her mother. And I promise you, sir, the next baby will be a boy."

The Admiral looked at him and said, "I already knew that."

"Yes, sir, I guess you'd already have known that." What could you say to someone that seemed to just know everything?

"If you decide to please my daughter, you just do it, don't you? And you know how to do so, too, don't you?" The Admiral seemed to be just thinking out loud, now. But the Admiral's eyes were a little moist as he gazed at his beautiful little granddaughter.

CHAPTER 60
NUPTIAL VOWS

Captain Ben Scott was waiting at the altar. Full Lieutenant Vic Mabry, his best man, was standing beside him. They both were wearing their formal dress uniforms. The march music started. They both looked over their shoulder to see a beautiful woman, dressed in white from her bare shoulders to her toes, come slowly marching down the aisle clinging to the arm of an elderly gentleman with white hair. He had on a black formal suit, complete with black bow tie and tails. The woman had khaki colored blonde hair. And she was beaming.

They were at the chapel at the main headquarters base at Seaside on the planet Ultaria. Lisa's father brought her to the alter and helped her up the steps to the platform. Then he turned to take his seat. Red took her place as matron of honor. The ceremony started. All was quiet in the little church as the two lovers made their nuptial vows. At the end of the ceremony, they slowly walked down the steps and marched down the aisle in time with the wedding music.

They planned to spend their honeymoon on Gorienth. Lisa had turned in her release of active duty forms. She had decided to get out of the Fleet Marines and just be a wife for a while. She wanted a baby. Ben had recently been promoted to Captain and had his own company, now. And he'd never been this happy. His new bride was still beaming when they climbed into Ben's rental gravity car. He'd have to buy Lisa a personal saucer, he knew. But they'd get by on a rental car for now.

* * *

Later that same month, a man in clean but rugged clothing and a woman in a new dress walked to the office of a Priest. The woman's dress was knee length, bright green and she was wearing green high heel shoes to match and she had a green ribbon in her hair. The man explained that they wanted to get married. The priest told them what the fee would be and that they would have to get a license. Jules had to get directions from him to the place where marriage licenses could be obtained. Then he and Nina went back to the Priest's office and the wedding ceremony was performed. The Priest's secretary signed the license as a witness. After the ceremony, Nina changed out of her high heel shoes into moccasins. They walked to the edge of town. They found a clump of bushes where they changed from their dress-up clothes into buckskins. Then Jules and Nina started their hike back to their mountain cabin that he had built during the past month. They'd have their honeymoon there.

* * *

A year later, far, far away, on the planet Oltaria, another wedding ceremony was being performed. Dan and Myrna stood before a minister and were exchanging wedding vows. Myrna's foreman gave the bride away wearing a bright red shirt, yellow bandana, a pair of new blue pants and shiny new riding boots. Dan wore a black suit with a black tie. Myrna was dressed all in white, of course.

At the end of Dan's 30 days leave on Myrna's ranch, he proposed to her. The following year when he came home on leave, he found all the barns full of hay and when he checked the books he saw that Myrna had made a nice profit the year he was gone. They decided to go ahead and set a wedding date during his leave. He had decided that he'd just never find another woman like her. So he decided to keep her.

Dan had decided to accept the life of a rancher with Myrna. He liked the wide open spaces. He had learned how to rope and ride and was making good progress learning how to be a cowboy. He could rope a running calf from the back of a galloping horse, now. He thought it would be a challenge that would keep him busy for some years. Of course, he had to complete his service obligation with the Fleet. But Myrna was happy to be married to him and just spend 30 days a year with him until then. And Myrna was simply in ecstasy. She was getting herself the most wonderful man in the world and getting to keep the life style she preferred as well.

CPSIA information can be obtained at www.ICGtesting.com
Printed in the USA
LVOW050706200213

320899LV00003B/10/P